DESTINY OF THE DRAGON PRINCE

ROYAL DRAGONS
BOOK ONE

SELINA COFFEY

LOVY BOOKS

ARISTA

"Arista, I don't have good news." The doctor came into the cold but well-lit exam room and stared down at me over the rim of his glasses. A man in his early fifties, with graying hair and kind eyes, he looked at me as though he was studying a bug.

"What do you mean?" I asked, my voice shaking with fear. Was it incurable cancer? Was I going to die?

"The tests all came back normal, Arista. Technically, there's nothing wrong with you." His voice was calm, but I could see his confusion.

I pushed honey-colored hair out of my brown eyes and stared at him. Again? This was happening again?

"But, you said you'd figure it out for me, Dr. Chang. You said you'd fix me when nobody else could." I tried to blink away tears but one fell anyway. I swiped at it like a child, hurt, angry, but most of all scared.

"I did promise that, Arista, and if I can figure out what's wrong I will fix it, but I don't know what else to do. I think, perhaps, we need to send you to a specialist or two." His shoulders slumped, and I felt sympathy for the good doctor. He'd tried.

He'd been my last hope, a man who had performed miracles for others, but he couldn't perform one for me.

"I'll think about it, Doc. Thanks." My own shoulders slumped. My illness sapped my strength but the doctor's news had defeated me.

I was going to die before anyone figured out what was wrong with me.

"Don't lose faith yet, Arista. Wait and see."

He didn't understand how most of my life was spent waiting. I waited for the pain in my head to stop so I could take a breath without feeling like my head was going to explode. I waited for my strength to return so I could take a bath. I waited for the nausea to pass so I could eat. Most of all, I waited for the day I'd feel normal again. I waited and longed for that day.

I murmured a thank you and left the exam room. I'd felt so much hope when I walked into the room twenty minutes before. After a year of decline and running out of hope, I'd found Dr. Chang through an online support group. He'd cured so many ailments that had gone undiagnosed that he was becoming a legend. Where other doctors only looked through the most common ailments then dismissed the patient as in need of mental health care, Dr. Chang went deeper and used all the resources available to him. He'd tried to do the same for me over the last month, but as with other doctors, he'd come up empty too.

No doctor could explain my sudden illness: the fatigue, migraines, and nausea that plagued me in the beginning. This had progressed to joint aches, swollen lymph glands, and my hair started to thin. Each day brought some fresh hell, and nothing was slowing it down. Now, as I stared into the tinted window of my car, I saw a woman with sallow skin beginning to show fine lines staring back at me. When I opened the car door I saw more evidence of my decline; my hands had developed the light-brown spots that generally came with age.

I was only twenty-three but looked like a woman in her late thirties, even her early forties, and nobody could explain why. Before my illness began, I'd been healthy, and some people even said I was freakishly strong. I was odd, always had been. But physically... well, I guess even physically I was odd.

People ignored my rather strange affinity for all things steampunk and Victorian, but it had been harder for them to ignore my strength. Even as a child of four, I'd had no problems lifting fifty-pound bags of dog food as though they were little more than a bag of popcorn. I wasn't allowed to play sports like soccer because I'd forget myself often and shoot the balls through the windows of my high school—a football field away—with the lightest of kicks. I'd learned to hide my strength but now that strength has left me. I thought about phoning my father, but he was on a business trip and I didn't want to disturb him. As I settled into the car and backed out of the clinic, an old thought returned. Maybe it was genetic, perhaps it was something my mother could shed some light on.

My parents divorced when I was nine years old and I haven't seen my mother since. Dad was given full custody of me, and because the courts considered my mom crazy, they'd not allowed visitation. I'd learned to stop asking Dad if I could see Mom a year after we moved away from the tiny little town of Drakeville, North Carolina, to the much more metropolitan city of Atlanta, Georgia. He'd get this pained look on his face when I asked, and his eyes would become distant. He'd always tell me that Mom was sick and needed help she wouldn't get. If she'd get help he'd let me see her, but until then I wasn't going back.

I'd grown up with only her memory and a lot of confusion. Mom would tell me great stories and we'd play together. She'd never hurt me or tried to take me away. I never understood what the problem was. So she liked to tell stories about dragons, we all have our quirks, right? I missed her, I missed my cousins, and I missed them deeply, but over time, I stopped trying to write her letters because they were never answered. I stopped thinking about her.

Dad didn't remarry, though he dated sometimes. It was just Dad and me, and after a while, I got used to it being that way. Dad was a contractor, one with a booming business, and most of the time his business partner did the traveling and late-night deals, which meant he could be home with me until I hit my teen years. I was always a good kid, I never caused trouble, and I'd spent most of my time studying things other kids found boring.

I went to college, earned a degree in communications and web design, then started my own business creating online games built around my hobby, mainly steampunk mystery games. I wasn't rich but I didn't have to rely on anybody else. Until I got sick, that is. I was still earning money from some of those games, but more and more I had to rely on my personal assistant and team to meet deadlines.

I hit the hands-free button when my phone began to ring and saw it was my dad.

"What did the doctor say, honey? Why didn't you call me?" His familiar voice filled my car as I pulled into the parking lot of my apartment building.

I smiled but it was tinged with sadness. "More tests, more doctors. The same old thing, Dad."

I heard him sigh over the line and tried to ignore it. I hadn't seen him in a few weeks, he'd been working a lot on a new project and I'd been stuck in bed.

"Honey, maybe all you need is more exercise? If the doctor isn't finding anything, maybe the other doctors were right. Maybe it's depression?" I could hear the doubt in his voice, the doubt that maybe I wasn't sick, and it angered me.

Over the last year, I'd been treated like a baby seeking attention, a drug addict seeking her next fix, and a hypochondriac. I'm sorry, but you know when you're ill and no matter how many times you're told you need a good dose of lithium, you know that isn't the answer.

"I can't believe you said that, Dad!" I was hurt, and I let him hear it in my voice. "After all I've been through, you're going to side with the people that would rather hand out a pill I'll be on for the rest of my life than cure me?"

"Now, Arista, you know I don't mean you're not ill. Depression can do a lot to a person, that's all." He sounded like he was trying to soothe a raging bull. I wasn't quite that angry, but I was upset.

"Like it did to Mom, you mean? You think I'm crazy too, is that it? Well you know what, Dad? Maybe you're right. In fact, I think I'll go and find out for myself just how crazy she is. Maybe it does run in the family!" I wanted to hang up on him now that I'd worked myself up, but I couldn't do that to my father, I loved him too much.

"Arista, you shouldn't do that. You've been gone a long time, you don't remember what it was like..." He cut himself off, and I knew what he'd left unsaid. Mom was insane, she believed dragons were real, he'd saved me from her lunacy.

I wasn't going to listen to it anymore.

"I'm a grown woman, Dad. I think it's time I see for myself just what kind of crazy Mom is. I've made up my mind. I'll call you before I leave."

But I didn't call him, I knew he'd just try to stop me. I packed a bag with the idea I'd head out that night but sat on the couch for a break and fell asleep. That was part of the problem with my illness, I grew tired very easily and the day had worn me out.

I woke up just as the sun began to rise, grabbed my bag, and headed out. I set up the navigation on my car and drove to the little village in North Carolina where I'd been born. I'd often looked it up online and knew the sad circumstances of the place. Once a farming community, Drakeville turned into a tourist beacon known for its forests and waterfalls, and for being near one of the tallest dams on the east coast. There were a few die-hard

Christmas tree farmers in the area, but not as many as there used to be, from what I read.

My mom's family had all been farmers, but Mom had escaped long enough to meet Dad at a university in Asheville before coming back home with a husband and a baby on the way. They'd both dropped out of school and lived in Drakeville, getting by, until Dad finally left Mom. I had no idea what Mom did now or even where she lived for sure. I knew in a village of 283 people one person would have to know her at the very least and would be able to tell me where she lived.

Maybe I even had cousins still living there? I hoped Willow was still there. She'd only been a few months younger than me, and I'd cried for her as much as I'd cried for my mom when Dad first took us away. We'd been inseparable from the time she came along, and people had often thought we were sisters. I could still remember her laugh and how we'd spent so much time giggling over boys and planning out our futures.

I drove for a little over three hours, heading north and slightly west into the Great Smoky Mountains. I saw some breath-taking views as I followed my sat-nav onto a scenic skyway, as the signs read. It didn't escape me that when we'd left only fourteen years before, cell phone towers didn't exist in the tiny village and the internet was only available to those that could afford a satellite package. I wondered if it was the same now.

I was near exhaustion when I drove into the village. I think every resident in the place turned to stare at me as I made my way to the only gas station on the one-way street. I stepped into the tiny shop and asked the woman there if she knew my mother.

"Eve? Of course, I know Eve. Why do you want to know where she lives?" The wizened face of the older woman with long gray hair combed tight against her head was twisted into a suspicious, squinty-eyed look that made me feel like I was guilty of some unknown crime.

"Well," I started quietly, my fingers twisting together as I looked around for something cheap to buy so she wouldn't be mad at me for just asking directions. The woman looked as though she very rarely smiled and that made me nervous. "She's my mother and I haven't seen her in a while. I'm not, well, I'm not exactly sure where she lives."

"You're Arista? Why, girl, you're all grown up! Let me look at you!" The woman came around the counter separating us, her face now a wreath of smiles. She was missing a few teeth, but she wasn't so intimidating with a smile on her face.

I looked at her tentatively, not sure who she was. A relative maybe?

"Girl, I haven't seen you since you was a little nipper! Look at you! Oh, now, I'm just going to have to see Eve's face when she sees you! She's waited so long to see you again! Come on, I'll lock the door and I'll take you up there. I'm Anne, your mom's cousin on her mom's side. I guess you don't remember me?" Her blue eyes looked at me for a moment, hoping for recognition, but I couldn't remember her at all.

"I'm sorry, it's been so long…" I was trying to be polite and not hurt her feelings. "I'm sure it'll come back to me."

"Oh, don't you worry about it girl, we'll all be familiar faces soon enough. Come on then." She led the way out, locked the door, and indicated that I was to follow her.

Anne jumped into an old long-bed truck with more rust than metal from the looks of it, and started down the street. She turned onto a road I wouldn't have seen if I'd passed it a dozen times, and we went upwards through a steep dirt road. I knew we were climbing the mountain and wanted to look around, but the road was so pitted I had to keep my eyes on it.

Mom hadn't lived out here when we left, so the move must have come after Dad took me away. We drove for about ten more minutes before we finally reached the top and I saw Mom's house. It was little more than a double-wide but it had a nice front porch on it and the views could take your breath away. Old maple trees stood around the place, keeping it shaded, and from what I could see, it was all kept neat and tidy.

A woman sat on a porch swing, one foot reaching out to keep up the motion and I knew right away who that woman was. Wrapped in a red blanket, my mother warded off the chill of the day as she waited for us to get out of our vehicles. She stood as I stepped out of the car, her eyes going wide in disbelief.

"Arista?" I could hear her whisper, and saw the tears in her eyes.

I'd been nervous on the drive up, wondering what she'd think of me, but now all I felt was love.

"Arista!" she cried out as she threw off the blanket and ran for me with open arms.

She was as tall as me and smelled of lemon-grass just like I remembered. I felt my knees go weak as she embraced me in a tight hug, and a sob escaped my throat. I'd thought I'd grown past the terrible pain of being away from her, my mother, the most adored woman in my life, but it all came crashing down on me then. Only now it was mingled with relief. I was in my mother's arms again and it felt so good.

"I've been waiting on you, honey," she whispered as she pulled away, her own face red and wet with tears. "I'm so glad to see you."

She placed her hands on my cheeks and just looked at me, and I gave her a watery smile. I was home at last.

2

ARISTA

My mom is crazy. Dad was right. I knew it later that evening, after our reunion and a nap in the room she'd prepared for me.

"They used to come into the villages, you know, steal the young women for breeding and kill off the men so they couldn't try to get the women back. They were terrible creatures, those dragons."

I watched her as she went through her normal routine whilst preparing dinner and wondered how a woman that looked so normal could be so damn crazy. From the way she chopped onions, to the careful way she measured out spices, you'd think she was as normal as the next person. She carefully went through each step as she prepared the sauce for a spaghetti dinner, and she looked fine. Clean and tidy with no weird expressions on her face. In fact, I remembered doing this every night before Dad took me away, poring over my homework as she cooked. Everything she did as she cooked brought back a memory of a stable mother I loved. It was her chatter that gave her away.

"Back in the old days, dragons were everywhere. There were werewolves and other kinds of shifters too. You know, people that can change into animals at will? Well it's not so common now, but back in the day, they were all over the place. Our family have always been dragon hunters. It's passed down the female line, you know?" I watched her, my mouth hanging open, as she went on.

"I don't know how it turned out that the women were the hunters. Maybe because the dragons kept killing off the men so the women had to find a way to defend themselves. Whatever happened, some of the women started to be born with powers. Great strength and the like. Like you, my darlin', with your strength. There were entire areas where women ruled, kind of like those Amazuns, I reckon."

She added her chopped vegetables to some heated oil as if she was having a normal conversation.

"That's why you're sick, I suppose, my darlin'. You've not been home, and this is where you belong. Our family came over here hundreds of years ago, after the dragons disappeared in England, and we've been in this area ever since. Your cousin, Willow, is ill too, did you know?" She glanced to where I was sat at the round pine table, and all I could do was shake my head in answer.

"Well, poor little thing, she's just as bad off as you are, Arista." She paused to put fresh pasta into boiling water. "I reckon it's some illness going around our kind. She and her mother will be here shortly, they couldn't wait to see you. You'll see for yourself that you aren't alone in this sickness business. Maybe the dragons have something to do with it. I wonder..." She tapped her chin before she picked up the spoon to stir the sauce.

After all these years, she was still going on about the dragons? I would have thought she'd have learned to stop talking about them when she lost me. At least she wasn't dangerous and unstable, she just seemed to believe in dragons like other people believed in fairies or religion. I wasn't like that. I lived my life in the real world, put my faith in things I could see and touch.

Maybe Dad had been right though, maybe my problem was mental. Maybe I'd inherited it from her.

The arrival of another car distracted me from my line of thought and I pushed myself up from the table in Mom's large open kitchen to go and greet the arrivals. I hadn't seen Willow since I was nine, and I was eager to see her despite how exhausted I felt. I made my way to the door and saw a young woman very similar to me in many ways, right down to the weary smile and tired lines around her eyes.

I held my arms out and we embraced softly, two sisters reunited after being separated for far too long. I held her close, but soon felt her mother's arms going around us both, then my own mother's. This is how it's supposed to be, I thought, as my family welcomed me home. Love, acceptance, no questions asked, just love. Even if we are all crazy.

"It's so good to have you home, Arista," Willow gushed as she pulled away at last. "I sure have missed you!"

I could only smile through more tears. Willow was my favorite and I'd missed her terribly. The whole day had seemed surreal and now was no different. I couldn't believe they were really here, any of them.

"I'm glad I finally came back to find you! I've just, well, I was busy and kept putting it off once I got out of school. I'm here now, though." I didn't want to get into it all, but I'd been afraid of coming back and being disappointed to find out Dad was right about Mom. I'd been right to wait, but I was concerned with how I'd found her.

At least now I could accept it.

"Come on through, ladies, dinner is almost ready." Mom waved us all toward her kitchen and we followed.

"How long are you staying? Have you come back for good?" Willow asked, her tired eyes still managing to shine with happiness.

"I'm not sure. I—"

Anne came in through the front door and interrupted, giving me an excuse not to finish. I wasn't sure how long I was going to stay, or if I even would.

Mom was crazy after all, and perhaps Dad was right. I still hadn't called him either, but Anne coming in stole my train of thought.

"I've found that drink you wanted, Eve. Took some doing, but I managed to order it." Anne handed over a glass bottle of some kind and put down a huge pack of bottled water. "This should keep you going for a while too."

Anne was gruff, as I already knew, and thick around the middle where Mom and my aunt Rachel were thin and delicate looking. She must have taken after her dad's side of the family because the rest of us all looked fairly similar. She was kind though, and despite my initial wariness of her, she'd won me over with gleaming blue eyes and her smile. I knew if I ever needed a defender or a friend, she'd be right there for me as she was for Mom.

"Thanks, Anne. I don't know what I'd do without you! I wish I'd learned to drive, but it was always so frightening to me, being in charge of something that could kill somebody else." Mom was stirring the pasta, testing whether it was time to come out, and her focus was on that.

"It's alright, Eve. I don't mind fetching for you, you know that. Now, did you make some garlic bread to go with that or am I going to have to slather some butter on some bread?" The older women gathered around, Rachel building a salad in a bowl, Anne checking the garlic bread in the oven, and Mom straining the pasta, while Willow and I watched them.

"They've done this their whole lives you know," Willow murmured, just loud enough for me to hear. "At least once a week, they get together over here. Your mom never did like to drive so they always came here."

"Did you know she'd kept a room for me?" It slipped out, I hadn't even been thinking about it, but the words came out anyway.

"She's waited a long time for you to come home, Arista, we all have. I'm just glad you're finally here." Her words ended with a sigh, and I could see the day was taking a toll on her as well.

I gripped her hand in mine, our bond still there after all the years that had separated us. "I'm glad I'm back too."

I didn't tell her I was worried about Mom, or that I was now afraid my dad might be right. I just held her hand and basked in the familial awesomeness taking place in front of me. Dinner went quickly enough, and we spent an hour catching up. Willow finished high school and got her cosmetology license. I told them about my job, and they all stared at me in wonder.

"So, you own your own business?" Mom asked, pride making her eyes shine.

"I do, yes. Speaking of, is there Internet up here now?" I looked around but didn't see anything like a computer or a router.

"No, we just use our phones up here." Aunt Rachel showed me her phone. "Although, I don't think your mom ever turns her's on."

They all laughed, and I saw Mom's cheeks go pink. "I just don't like those things. I'll call down to Collette tomorrow if you need something like that, Arista. Whatever you need to keep you working, honey."

"Thanks, Mom." I was curious what she did for a living, but I didn't ask. She might get some kind of public assistance and I didn't want to embarrass her. I'd pay for whatever I needed, though.

"I'm going to get Willow home, ladies. Her eyes are drooping." Aunt Rachel put the dish towel she'd been using over a hook and turned to the table.

"Arista looks like that nap of hers wasn't long enough. Anne, are you staying for coffee?" Mom kept chattering as we all got up from the table.

"I believe I will, Eve, if you don't mind. Rachel, it was good to see you again."

We all said our goodbyes and I went back to my

room and pulled a set of pajamas out of my bag. Mom had decorated the room with a double bed, a chest of drawers to accompany the closet, two pine end tables with white ceramic lamps, and a desk. My desk from when I was little. All my things were there, and I knew she'd brought everything from the old house with care. It was sweet and touched me deeply.

I was tired, exhausted even after my nap, and wanted to get into the bed quickly. A noise outside drew my attention, and I walked over to the white linen curtain hanging over my bedroom window. It sounded like a woman screaming but even after all these years, I knew it was a mountain lion. I glanced out of my window and quickly shut the curtain again.

That didn't just happen. I didn't just see a woman turn into a wolf out there. Did I? I glanced back out of the window again but there was nothing there. It was my imagination! It had to be.

I walked away from the window and went to the bed. I was going to have to face facts, I might just be losing my mind. If it runs in the family, it wouldn't be a surprise. Imagine, thinking you saw a woman turn into a wolf! I'll be blathering on about dragons with Mom next.

I tucked the covers under my chin and closed my eyes, not letting myself think about my imagination. I was worried I'd keep myself awake, but I was asleep soon enough. A long morning of driving, the emotional roller coaster of meeting so many people again, and my illness won out over my brain. I'd call Dad tomorrow, I thought, before sleep took me. Maybe I'd even tell him he was right. Not right to take me away from Mom, but definitely right about her being crazy. Dragons, indeed.

3

MALCOLM

"Where are we, Mary?" I stared around at a variety of trees, the smell of wood smoke slightly tinting the air.

"I think this place is called North Carolina, Mal." My sweet sister's voice came in a whisper, but there was no need. Humans wouldn't be able to see us, but she must have felt the same need as I did to protect ourselves in this unknown territory.

"I guess there's a south in this land of Carolinas then." I brushed hair out of my eyes and looked around. I was letting the blond locks grow out again. It annoyed my father, but right now they were more annoyance to me than to him.

Mary and I were hunting a wolf, one that was trying to abscond with a child belonging to panther shifter parents. We needed to be on our guard and be careful, not busy pushing hair out of our eyes. Mary handed me a soft circlet of velvet and I gaped at her.

"What am I supposed to do with this, Mary? Offer the man kinky games?" I made to put the small piece of material in my pocket, but she sighed and rolled her eyes. She was never afraid to speak her mind around me, the heir to the throne our father would one day vacate.

"Tie your hair up with it, you numpty!" Mary gave an exasperated sigh, her green eyes giving away her annoyance.

I turned away, not wanting to laugh while we were searching for a kidnapper, but her annoyance amused me. She was always trying to come across as hard, as one of the boys, but she was too cute. I still saw the little girl with pink cheeks even when she was glaring at me.

"I might be a numpty, Mary, but I'm not a brat. Like some people I know." I rolled my own gray eyes at her antics when she stuck her tongue out at me and walked through a line of trees. I paused when I caught a scent from a slight breeze. There were wolves about. "This way."

We could have shifted back into our dragon forms and flown over the wooded land, but we needed to be on the ground to catch this guy. We weren't often in this part of the world, there may even still be dragon hunters in this backward area Mary had tracked the wolf to.

Those menacing female figures hadn't haunted us for generations now, but one never knew in the wilds of unknown territories. I scoffed at myself quietly, imagine dragon hunters existing after all this time.

"Why has he chosen to run to the human world? Why put himself at risk like that?" I was thinking out loud, albeit in a loud whisper to Mary.

"I suppose he could be trying to avoid our world. He knows that if he stays in our world, in our land, he'll be caught. Maybe that's why he's come to this New World." She was behind me, climbing up a mountain that might rival some of the hills in our magical part of England, though it wasn't really England.

That bit was hard to explain. Our land existed around, but on top of the human world, and went unseen by the humans. I suppose it could be called a parallel universe, I pondered as I corrected her.

"I think it's called the United States now."

"Of course it is, Mal. I only meant it is a new world to us in the real world. This human world is new, isn't it? Especially this part of it." She sounded irritated, and I grinned. I was getting to her then. Getting Mary's goat was one of my favorite pastimes, mainly because it was so easily done.

"Well, to be fair, we're new to both worlds in the grand scheme of things. I'm only thirty-two and you're thirty. It's all old to us."

"Mal. I will emasculate you with a twig," Mary warned, her tone telling me she'd about had enough of me tonight.

"Do you think they consider *their* world the real world?" I carried on as if she hadn't threatened me.

"Mal! Shut your trap!" Mary was really getting angry now. I gave a cheeky but quiet laugh and continued traipsing up the hill.

Our world, the world of vampires, shifters, and other creatures the humans considered monsters, left the human realm around the time electricity and the telephone were invented. Communications were improving and where we used to be able to hide in a world where stories rarely made it out of small towns and mountain dwellings, tales of monsters could now spread quickly. We'd left this newly threatening world to the humans and built our own around it to protect us all.

"There's something up here, Mal, look."

I turned around to see Mary pointing in the other direction from where I'd been looking.

A small, odd home was nestled on the top of the hill, protected by overhanging pine and maple trees. A light was on somewhere in the home, but the rest were off.

"I don't think that's it. Let's keep looking. The place doesn't smell of shifters." I glanced back at the little house one last time. Something about the place drew me.

The wind shifted and I caught a much stronger scent this time. "This way."

I swerved around a small building a good distance from the house and kept my nose in the air. The scent was getting stronger the lower down I went. Mary and I moved quietly on dragon-made boots. The leather soles were thick but soft, matching the suede that ran up to our knees to offer protection. Dressed in black pants with long black coats, the uniform of my father's security force—the Dragon Guard—we blended into the shadows. We were little more than shadows and if a human saw anything of us it would be only a shadow. They would hear only the whisper of a breeze as we moved over the rocky ground.

As my father's heir and head of his security force, only my father was more powerful than me. As dragons, we were at the very top of the food chain anyway. Normally, I would be back at my father's castle, making sure he was safe and well protected, but he'd insisted I be the one to find the child. It seemed nobody else measured up in my father's view, and he had faith I would find the child alive and well.

For now, my concentration was occupied with the scent of the wolf we were tracking. They'd stolen the newest cub of one of my father's servants. The servant was one of my father's favorites and my father had sent Mary and me out to retrieve it, as well as the thief.

"What's driving them to steal children? Are our numbers that low now?" I was aware our numbers were falling, we hadn't had any new recruits in over three years, but had it grown that bad? Normally, no one would dare cross my father, but the act of taking a child was in itself a scream to us all that something was wrong.

"It's getting fairly dire, Mal. I can't quote numbers but I know that more and more females aren't producing. Out of five of my friends that have mated, only one has produced a child. It's happening all over our world." She paused to climb over a boulder as we neared a clearing at the bottom of the hill.

I stopped her, and we hunkered down behind the rock to look around. "So, people are stealing children now to make up for it? But why steal a panther child if you're a wolf?"

"I heard Will's wife is desperate. She's lost a few pregnancies now, and honestly, I think she's become unstable. He's attempting to appease her."

"That must be heartbreaking for her, to lose so many children." I might be a man that people would not cross, but I did have a heart.

"Yes, I suppose it is. We dragons might only be the tip of the iceberg when it comes to shifters, but we own that iceberg, and we are the rulers. The problem is going to have to be investigated and dealt with. That might even be the plan with this kidnapping. They wanted our attention and now they have it." Mary sounded miffed.

"Why are you so angry?" I inquired, turning to her momentarily. She rarely showed anger at others.

"Father should have had a team on this a long time ago, when the numbers first started to drop. He was content to let it drop because our world was starting to get a bit crowded. Now we're in danger of not having enough young to replace all the jobs we have to fill."

"Ah, I understand. All the walls in the world are pointless if there's nobody to hide behind them?" I said.

"That's it exactly. Now come one, I think he's close."

We ended up hiking further down the valley, along a natural stream that ran through it, before we found their camp. As dragons, we were able to mask our smell from others, and because of our training, Mary and I were both stealthy. We were on them before they knew it, but we paused, gathering information.

"We have to take him back, Eric. He's not ours!" A pretty, black-haired wolf female in her late twenties was sitting on a log in front of a campfire, staring into the flames as her husband tended the fire from her side.

"We can't take him back, Amy! They'll catch me, and if they don't hang me, they'll put me in jail for the rest of my life. I thought this was what you wanted!" The husband, in his late thirties, looked at his wife, consternation marring his features.

"I do want a child, Eric, but *our* child. Not a baby you stole!" The woman wasn't being quiet, and I could see how agitated she was as she rocked the baby. Her whole body moved, not just her arms.

I didn't think either of the wolves was dangerous, but desperate people did stupid things. I waited to find out all we could before we took them and lost the chance at candid moments like this.

The man put his arm around his wife and kissed the top of her head. "He's ours now, Amy. As long as we can keep away from the dragons, anyway."

He looked around, as if checking, but he didn't see us, as I knew he wouldn't. We were completely cloaked behind the rock.

"What's his name, Eric?" She looked down at the baby in her arms, wrapped in a soft green blanket.

"I think we should give him a name, Amy. Change it you know? Aelfric is going to stand out in this world."

"I don't know, Eric, have you seen what they name their kids in this world? Champagne? Since when is that a name?" She laughed.

"True, but even that stands out. What about Seth? I like that one."

"If that's what you want, Eric."

I tried not to shift too much, but this wasn't the kind of information I needed. I wanted to know if anyone helped him do this.

"Let's get you two to bed, Amy. We have to decide where to put the house tomorrow. I think we need to stay away from that stream, it won't always be so small, but we should stay fairly close to it."

They were planning on staying here then. If the child in Amy's arms wasn't stolen, and if Eric hadn't kidnapped the child of my father's favorite servant, what Mary and I were about to do would be heartbreaking. I had to steel myself. The woman would scream, the man would try to defend her and the child. I didn't want to do this.

It was my job, though. This is one of the reasons I was going to be king one day. I could do the things others couldn't force themselves to do. Like take back a child that was so wanted but stolen. The child belonged with its parents, not these people. This was not the way to get a child. That was a problem for another time though, now was the time to retrieve the child and take it back to the parents that adored it. Then deal with the fallout.

I signaled to Mary and we moved out of the shadow of the boulder. The woman gave a low cry of fear and the man stood, his fists up and ready. He knew he was defeated, that's why his fists came up instead of shifting to his more powerful wolf form. His fists were up for the cuffs he knew I was going to wrap around his wrists.

I was a dragon. He had no hope of escaping.

"I knew we couldn't run," the man, Eric, said as his shoulders slumped. "I'm sorry, Amy. I tried, my love."

"We'll try to make this easy for you, Eric, but you know you'll have to pay the consequences." I walked up to him, put the cuffs on him and gave Amy a moment to compose herself.

Her hiccups turned into outright sobs, though, once Eric was cuffed. "He was only doing it for me, Malcolm. Can't I go in his place?"

"No, Amy!" Eric cried out, refusing to hear more of that. He went up a little more in my estimation.

"No, he's right, Amy. Eric took the child, not you." Besides, she might be able to carry a child at some point, being in prison with a bunch of other women wasn't going to make that happen.

If our numbers were dwindling, we needed more children. Putting Amy in prison too wouldn't help that. No, she'd go back to her life. I didn't know what would happen to Eric, but I would speak with my father about it. This wasn't a malicious act, not like kidnap and ransom anyway, but a desperate act. A man trying to give his mate what she wanted the most. He'd just made a rather huge mistake trying to deliver it.

Mary shifted and took Amy and the baby on her back to fly them home. I kicked out the fire and gathered their things before I turned back to Eric, who stood with his head hanging in defeat.

"I'll talk to my father for you, Eric. It's all I can do." I didn't know the man, I only knew his name because his wife had spoken it, but I knew he wasn't evil, not really.

"I'm sorry, Malcolm." Our people knew my name, my face, it was as famous as my father's in our world.

"Love will make you do stupid things, Eric. Or so I've heard." I didn't have a mate, so I didn't know.

"It'll tear your heart out and serve it back up to you on a platter," Eric ground out, his eyes going to the sky. "Stupid doesn't even begin to cover it."

"Thanks for not running further, that would have been even worse. I would have had to kill you then." I said it with a jocular tone, but I wasn't joking.

I shifted then, and he climbed onto my back, settling into the natural dip between my shoulders. He'd be safe there, and there'd be no danger of him falling out.

I flew us back to our own realm, dragon speed cutting the flight to a fraction of the time it took a plane to fly across the Atlantic. I'm sure Eric wished it was longer, but I'd done my job. Now it was time for him to face the music.

I landed on the big red circle we used as a landing pad and marched Eric to the prison. A panther was the jailer. His face told me he was happy we'd managed to get the child back, but Eric would pay dearly for it.

"He is not to be touched, Gerald," I warned the other man, a menacing tone in my voice.

"But, Malcolm!" he began, but I wouldn't let him finish.

"No. Untouched. Or you all pay; do you understand me?" I could all but feel my jaw popping from how hard I had it clenched. "He fucked up but that doesn't mean you kill him. Or harm him in any way, do you understand?"

"Yes, Malcolm," the guard said, and ducked his head.

He knew what my punishment would be if I wasn't obeyed and he didn't want to face that. I didn't play around, anyone that disobeyed me ended up in a desert, whether that was a desert of sand or ice, was down to my whim of the moment.

"That's all I can do for you, for now, Eric. I'll see my father when I can." I clapped the other man on the shoulder and Gerald took him away.

I'd done my job. That's all I could do.

4

ARISTA

"What do you mean you're at your mother's? I thought we discussed this?" My father wasn't a happy camper.

That was three hours and four coffees ago, and I hadn't heard anything from him since his final words to me.

"I'll be there shortly."

Now, instead of napping like I wanted to, I was busy watching the window in Mom's living room. I wanted to cut him off before she saw him, before he broke her heart again. After a week of being with Mom, I knew she still loved Dad, she just didn't understand why he thought she was crazy or why he'd taken me away. She was proud of how I'd turned out despite her not being around, but she was still hurt.

I could understand. I was hurt I'd lost that bond with

her. Dad did what he thought was best for all of us, I could understand that too, but I was a grown woman now. Not a child that needed permission to see her own mother. Why he thought he needed to come here was beyond me. I'd worked up a rather righteous anger by the time I heard a car coming up the hill. I went out and sat on the front porch swing I'd first seen Mom sitting in when I came.

Dad pulled into the driveway and I could only watch from the porch. My pulse raced and I chewed at my lip. What was he going to say? I thought he might be angry with me. After all, I'd left without calling him. I was just as angry that he'd followed me up here. Dad and I had been in arguments before but this was different, mainly because it involved Mom. There was also the fact that I'd ignored him when he told me not to come up here.

Dad stepped out of the car, his face set in a grim expression. This wasn't going to be a happy greeting then.

"Hi, Dad," I said, staying on the porch and not greeting him with my usual hug. That probably tipped him off that I was angry, because he didn't come up on the porch to give me one either.

"Arista, why are you here? You shouldn't be around your mother. She's not healthy." He rubbed at his face, a face that I knew as well as my own.

"She might not be totally sane, I get that, I mean,

what are those dragons about?" I trailed off but soon picked up the thread again. "She isn't dangerous though."

"No, I don't think she's dangerous now. When you were young and impressionable, she might have been a negative impact on your mental health, but not now. Now I'm just worried you're going to get hurt. It's one thing having people tell you one of your parents is crazy, it's another thing to witness it." His eyes pleaded with me for understanding, and I turned away.

His words hit too close to the truth. "Dad, I'm twenty-three, I'm a big girl now, I can deal with her mental illness. I can't deal with not having answers. The doctors couldn't give me the answers, you couldn't give me answers, so now I've turned to Mom. She's my last hope."

"Baby girl, you won't find answers here. I believe you need a psychiatrist. If your doctors couldn't find an answer then maybe you're mentally ill too. There's no shame in that."

"No shame? Weren't you ashamed of her when you took me away? No, I suppose there wasn't any shame for her, you were too busy carrying all of that around for her. She doesn't see anything wrong with thinking dragons are real. You do, though. You divorced her, had her declared unfit, because you were ashamed your wife believed in dragons." My voice had started to rise and over a decade of anger suddenly poured out of me, leaving me feeling weak.

I slumped back down to the swing and stared at him. "You left her, you took me away, and yet you tell me there's no shame in mental illness?"

"That's not what I meant. It wasn't about being ashamed either. I meant..." He paused, swiping at his face again. "I just meant you can't help being mentally ill, you can only get through it."

"That's not helping, Dad." I squinted my eyes at him. "So now we've gone from I *might* be mentally ill to I *am* mentally ill? That's just great."

His eyes went wide and I could see the panic on his face. I felt bad for giving him a hard time but he'd made his bed a long time ago. He'd taken me away and I hadn't realized just how angry I was about that until I saw him pull into the driveway.

"You messed up, Dad. Coming here now only brings that home to me. You messed up because you didn't like the fact that your wife believed in fairy tales. Now you want to break up what I've only just begun to rebuild? You want to take away the last chance I have of finding an answer?"

"Honey, you aren't going to find answers here, not from your mother." His voice was pleading again, asking me to see reason.

I couldn't though, not with these lines around my eyes and exhaustion as a constant companion.

"Then don't I deserve a little bit of time with the mother you denied me? Don't I deserve that much? I don't know how much longer I have before I can't get out of bed at all. I think I deserve just a little more time with my mother. You had me to yourself for over fourteen years, Dad. Let me have this time now."

For once, he was speechless. The man who had an answer to everything finally had nothing to say.

"Alright, Arista. But if you get worse…"

"I'm already worse, Dad. Look at me." I held my hands out, holding the blanket I'd covered myself with open.

My pajamas sagged on my frame, though they were meant to be snug. He'd got them for me for Christmas, so he knew they were far too big now. It was like he was only just seeing how ill I was. His eyes scanned my face, saw the lines, the way my hair was thinning, and how pale I looked. He really saw it now, and I knew he did because he was stunned.

"Arista, I need to take you to a hospital. You need to eat. Are you not eating? Is that it?"

I sighed and closed my eyes, trying to calm myself. "I'm eating, Dad. I'm eating enough for three people some days. I can't always keep it down, and the other days I can't eat at all. Some days it's because I don't have the strength, other days it's because I'm too nauseous. But yeah, maybe you're right, maybe it is all in my head and I just need to take a pill to make it all better." I paused to let him truly take me in before I finished. "I think you should go, Dad. Go back home."

I started to turn around and walk back in the house, but Mom chose that moment to come outside. I'd talked her into taking a nap, but I guess our arguing woke her up. "Mom…"

"Who's here, baby?" She wiped at her eyes sleepily, a smile on her face until she looked around me and saw Dad.

"Ted?" She looked at my father, his blond hair now more gray than blond, and it was like the years melted away.

Her face somehow went smooth when she smiled, and I saw the woman he must have fallen in love with all those years ago. Wow, she was really beautiful.

"Eve. Um, sorry to intrude. I wanted to see Arista." He couldn't take his eyes off her and it was amazing to watch. He'd really loved her, I could see that now.

I'd always known he was hurt when he left Mom, that it wasn't something he'd done lightly, but in that glimpse of adoration before he schooled his features into a placid mask of composure, I saw how he really felt.

"Why don't you come in?" Her voice was sweeter,

softer than it was when she talked to me or anybody else in the family. It was a sound from my past, but only a vague one.

"I've got to get back into town, find somewhere to sleep tonight. I'll call you later, Arista."

He all but ran from us both then, his eyes glued to the ground. I don't think I've ever seen him move so fast.

"Ted…" Mom called after him, but he was in his car and gone before she could finish. I watched sadness move across her face like a storm cloud and wanted to throw a rock at my dad. He'd just broken her heart. Again!

"Come in the house, Mom," I said, wrapping my arm around her shoulder as though she were the invalid and not me. "We'll get some dinner going, shall we?"

She let me lead her back into the house and we spent the evening quietly together, watching old movies on television. She liked the black and white romance films and I didn't have it in me to tell her I hated romance films. If I learned anything from them both, it was that true love didn't last, no matter how much you want it to.

She made me her grandmother's chicken and dumplings recipe, the kind with big fluffy dumplings rather than the flat noodle-like ones I was used to. That seemed to make my tummy happy and I even had some energy later that evening. Later, I decided to walk around her little version of the top of the world, to see what it looked like in moonlight.

I found myself humming an old song from one of the movies we'd watched earlier and smiled. A slight breeze blew, bringing a scent of pine with it. The breeze was warm, rather than cold, and I found it odd, but I hadn't been in the mountains for a long time. Maybe that was normal up here.

I looked up at the moon and thought about my parents and how they'd reacted to each other today. I'd seen the love there, before hurt hid Mom's and anger hid Dad's. They'd loved each other dearly for so long, why had Dad suddenly decided that he couldn't take the dragon thing?

Maybe that was my purpose here, to bring them back together. Maybe that's what had really driven me home, not just a need for answers, but an attempt to right a wrong. How could I do that? I wondered as I walked along. A scent hit me, distracting me from my thoughts.

It was a smell that pulled at a hunger deep within me. I tried to follow it, my strength coming back amazingly fast the longer I followed. I felt a longing unlike anything I'd ever felt before when I smelled that scent, but it was one I'd never smelled before. I followed it along the edge of the mountaintop, down to a stand of maple trees.

A loud swishing noise made me shriek and jerk back

to the safety of the moonlit mountaintop. I saw something large in the sky, but it flew to a cloud before I could make out the exact shape of the creature. It must have been a very large bird. That was all.

I walked back towards the house, feeling some of my renewed strength ebbing away. What had that thing been? And what was the smell it produced? It was something like pine, but that might have just been the trees. There was some smell beneath that, something that made me think of only one word… desire.

I'm not a pure as the driven snow kind of girl, but I wasn't one to normally think in terms of desire. Lust maybe, arousal, yes… but desire? Just not in my mental vocabulary. Yet, it was all I could think of now.

I went back to my room, and for the first time in a long time, took out the laptop I'd built my games on. I had some energy and wanted to use it while I could. As I built a world of steam-powered, clockwork gadgets, I tried to get the whole thing out of my head.

I was working on a scene in an abandoned room when a previous thought intruded again. Maybe Dad was right. Maybe I was crazy.

5

MALCOLM

"I have found a nest of dragon hunters. What are your orders?" I read the note and squinted at it. Dragon hunters?

With a flick of my hand, the paper disappeared, incinerated in an instant. We had use of the human gadgets that came our way at times, but we didn't need cell phone towers and Wi-Fi to communicate. We used pieces of paper because they could be destroyed instantly, couldn't be retrieved later, and weren't as vulnerable to interception as so-called digital communications were. Sometimes the old ways were better.

I considered the words and decided that it was a matter my father would want to know about, though I scoffed at it. Dragon hunters? Even if they were really the fabled female hellions from our past, their blood would be so diluted by now that they probably didn't even know what they were.

I pulled out the earphones in my ears and hid them in my clothes. My father hated human gadgets, which was another reason we didn't use them. He'd really hate it if he knew I wasn't listening to our music, but old honky-tonk country from the era the humans called the 1980s. It was one of the many things I kept hidden from my father. I liked a broad range of music, but I always tended to wander back to the Americans and their twangy songs about drinking and heartbreak. Something about it appealed to me.

I ducked through the doorway of my room and walked through the sandstone walls of the castles, headed for my father's day chambers. He wouldn't be in the throne room, that was only used on special occasions. I soon arrived at the room and pushed through a herd of men standing around and murmuring unhappily. They sounded like a bunch of old chickens, clucking over a new hen's first egg, that were afraid of being turned into dinner.

"Malcolm, have you received the news?" My father, a few inches taller than me, had black hair rather than my blond, but I knew exactly where my eyes came from. Cold as steel, his gray eyes saw me before I'd even managed to get three feet into the door.

"What news is that, Father?" I asked, stepping up to

the wide writing desk where my father sat, every inch the king in his domain.

From his hard jaw to his cold eyes and strong hands, my father was *the* king. One day, I'd be the one to take his place, but that would be centuries from now. My father was only 336, after all, still a young dragon.

"This rumor about dragon hunters. Did you know about this little enclave in the New World?" My father was a lot like Mary, both refused to see America as a land as old as ours. My father's reasons were different from Mary's though. He considered the magical world of the original inhabitants of that land to be younger because they weren't "discovered" until Europeans came to intrude on them. Hence, the *new* world.

"I've only just had a note about it, Father. What are your wishes?" I studied him, wondering how he'd deal with this threat.

"Kill them all." My father stared directly into my eyes as he spoke, leaving little room for argument. "Their blood is impure by now, so there should be no fight left in them. Kill every last one of them, before they accidentally breed a real hunter."

My father wasn't always a ruthless man, but when it came to threats to our way of life, to our people, he could be the most dangerous being on earth. I tilted my head in acknowledgment of his words and made to leave. Father stopped me, however.

"Every one of them, Malcolm. Even their whelps." His eyes drilled into me again and I felt it, almost like a blow.

"Yes, Father." He said it like he hadn't just ordered me to kill living, breathing humans. I'd have more blood on my hands just for him.

I was a soldier, the head of his security force, blood did not frighten me, but I sometimes wondered if there would ever come a time when all of that blood would haunt me. It wasn't so bad when it was the nasty little trolls that liked to set fire to the houses on the outskirts of our town, but humans had a pitiful death scream that sometimes made my gut twist. Even when that scream was only a sigh of breath, it still sounded like a scream to me.

This wasn't going to be a fun little raid that ended with drinking and sex, it was going to be one that ended with me staring into flames until the screams stopped playing in my head.

I saw my brothers and only sister waiting on me as I left the room, their gear already in bags on their backs. I wanted Mary to stay home, she didn't need to have this on her heart, but I saw the set of her jaw and knew she'd argue.

"I want to go too, Mal," she started in right away. "You can't turn me away. I'm not a little girl anymore."

"That might be so, Mary," I started wearily, this

wasn't a new argument. "But you are Father's only daughter, and that means you should be here, preparing to be married off to some king far away."

"I'm not that kind of girl, Mal. You know that." She met my eyes steadily and I knew she was right. She was as tough and useful as our brothers. I could use her level-headed observation skills on this task.

"Fine. You stay with me, though." I glared at her until I saw her cave and back down a little.

We were all dressed in the black leather uniform of the security team, so we went out to the flight pad to begin our journey. One by one we all shifted, matching black dragons with red markings. Mary was the largest, oddly enough, a feat I think she accomplished through sheer will, just to show us up. She was even larger than Tristan, the only member of our team not one of my siblings.

He wasn't as tall as my two brothers, but he dwarfed Mary. He was as handsome as the rest of us, but that wasn't why I'd chosen him. He was good at what he did, blond hair and blue eyes be damned. Henry was the second son, only a couple of months younger than me. Irish twins, I suppose. He had Father's black hair and our mother's green eyes. Aleric, the youngest of us all, was the odd one out, with blond hair and the blue eyes of our paternal grandfather. Otherwise, he was the spitting image of our father too.

We'd all shifted to our dragon forms—Tristan black with green tints, rather than our black and red—and took flight. We flew in a v-pattern until we were close. My brother Aleric acted as navigator by flying in the midpoint of the v, leading us all. He was the youngest at twenty-nine, but his navigational skills were inherent. He could find the most remote place in the world just by glancing at a map and taking off. He must have been given directions before we left.

I saw Aleric begin to shrink as he flew to a place that was familiar to me. This was the area the wolf had run to a few days before. The place that had drawn me, but I hadn't come back yet to explore what might have caught my attention. I'd been far too busy to come back. Was that what it was, some intuition that had picked up the scent of a huntress?

We all followed his lead and reduced our size. We could shift down to smaller sizes, and larger, but we all had a maximum size and it always amused me that Mary was larger than all of us. Female dragons were usually smaller, more delicately boned than us men. Mary showed us all up.

Aleric flew down to a tall pine tree and we all found a branch to settle on. We were no bigger than crows now, though still in dragon form. Any human eyes that saw us would merely see a flock of birds. A murder, I think it's called, a group of crows. Apt considering what we were there to do.

I saw a home through the trees but didn't sense anything immediately, so flew to another tree further up the mountain. I paused as the others joined me on an outcrop of rock. I couldn't make out much through the trees, but something was buzzing in my head, the further up the mountain I flew. I had an excellent memory and knew this was the mountain with the house on it.

I took flight once more, my long tail trailing out behind me. I followed the buzzing as it grew inside of my ears, an odd sensation of joy but irritation making my eyes roll. What was this? I had felt something the last time, but nothing quite like this. I kept flying in that direction, wondering if this was a built-in warning system. We were hunting dragon hunters, perhaps this was an ancient, inherent sense coming to life.

Whatever it was, it was about to drive me to distraction. I had to stop as we came near the house, the buzzing was just too much. I looked at the others and saw there were only curious stares. Why had I stopped again? Their silent question hung in the air.

I hissed a sound that translated to "wait" to them. I put my dragon hands on my head, knowing it wouldn't help. What was this noise? I was on the verge of screaming as the buzzing continued to get more powerful, but then it stopped, just as I heard the others around me hiss all at once.

I looked up, relieved that it was over, confused as to what had happened, but curious. Why had they all given off a warning hiss?

I saw a woman coming from the house, small and human, but just the sight of her made my blood surge in my veins. I could smell her, even from this distance, and knew what that smell meant. Sweet, alluring, and intoxicating. This was my mate.

She walked out of the house, off the porch, and into the trees close to where we perched. The others were shifting on their perches, tracking her movements. She'd caught their attention for some reason. I knew why she'd caught mine, she was my mate. I knew it as well as I knew what hunger felt like.

She was ill, her body growing weak without me near her, but she wasn't beyond saving yet. It was an attribute of the mating phenomenon when our mates were not shifters, the weaker human would die if they did not find their mate. We shifters, protected by our strength, would only weaken after we'd physically mated if we were ever separated. I'd always wondered if I'd find my mate.

It didn't always happen. Sometimes shifters gave up and married, especially if they felt like they were in love. Being mated was far different to mere love. It was a bond that was almost physical, though invisible, and went far deeper than love. Mates were for life, and she was mine.

I felt desire surge through my body, followed by anger when a wolf launched itself from the woods and onto the woman, knocking her over. The woman screamed and fell to her knees before the wolf knocked her to the ground by pouncing on her back. I flew down, like an arrow loosed from a bow, and pushed the wolf away.

Chaos took over from there, I heard snarls as my team flew down from the trees, shouts from the frightened woman, and a few loud curses as two more wolves came from the trees to defend their pack mate. I squared off with the one that had attacked the woman, letting my size increase until the wolf knew it was beaten and cowered on the ground.

I stared him down, my anger urging me to tear his throat out, but I knew we needed answers. Smoke billowed from the tip of my nose and the wolf whimpered, knowing he could be blasted into infinity in a moment.

"Why are you attacking this human?" I demanded once I'd shifted into my human form. My team did the same, the three wolves now all low to the ground in submission.

I glanced over to see the woman on the ground, her

eyes round and huge in her face. She was safe for now, and by the look on her face, too stunned to move. Besides, I knew where she lived if she ran off. I could tell her strength was coming back already, my presence gave her the gift of healing, but she was still too weak to run far.

I turned back to the wolf, my eyebrow crooked at him. "Well? Why are you attacking humans? You know it is forbidden. They can turn, and that endangers us all. Not all humans are capable of keeping our world hidden."

"We need mates that can breed, Mal! The number of women in our pack is dwindling." He'd shifted to answer me, but he shut up when one of his pack nipped his leg. "It's no use, George. It's happening all over the shifter world, keeping it secret isn't an option anymore. There are fewer women, and even fewer that can breed successfully."

"More of this. Right, team, you know what to do with them. At least this one here." I pointed at the one that had attacked the woman. "As for the other two, technically we did not see them commit a crime, but it will be up to Father to decide what to do with them. They were planning to help him and Father is the ulti-mate decider in our world."

I gave the wolf a pointed look and I knew he under-stood when his shoulders sagged. His clan might have a leader, but my father ruled above even that leader. The wolf would pay the price for breaking our ultimate law and he knew it.

That's when he shifted and pounced at her again, his claws going out to swipe at her leg.

6

ARISTA

It had been a normal day, as normal as it would get at my mother's house, that is, and I was answering some emails that couldn't wait any longer when I smelled that scent again. Then I felt a sudden surge of energy like I had before. I got off my bed and looked around.

I don't know what I was looking for, but I could feel life flooding back into me as the scent lingered in the air. That had to mean something, right? That I was bonkers, more than likely, I thought to myself as I went out onto the porch. What if I wasn't crazy, though? I squinted into the darkness, but I couldn't see anything.

The scent was stronger out here in the open, and it smelled so good. It was like chocolate, hot buttered popcorn, love, desire, warm brownies, and apple pie, all mixed together, with the scent of pine thrown in for good measure. Beneath all of this was the scent of a man —that unique smell that could be a cologne but is really a natural scent.

I walked towards the woods, towards the smell that was so incredibly provocative.

Why do we try to mask that? I started to wonder, when something launched itself at me out of the darkness and I tumbled to the ground. I didn't have time to do anything more than scream when it stamped down onto my back and I felt the hot breath of some beast, teeth bared and poised to pierce into my neck if I moved.

I wanted to scream for my mother's help, I wanted to turn over and fight the animal off, but its teeth were right on the delicate skin at the back of my neck. The animal growled at me when I tried to move and pressed one paw deeper into my right shoulder, pinning me to the ground.

I felt the exhaustion slipping away, and power surging back into me. Far more power than I'd ever felt I had before. The beast yelped and the weight disappeared. I rolled over quickly, taking a natural defensive stance, albeit from the ground, and watched the unthinkable happen.

A tiny little dragon grew bigger, until the wolf cowered before it. I considered if straight-jackets came in a variety of colors or just white. Then more stepped out of the darkness and all I could do was stare. That was where the scent was coming from: the dragon. I could smell it stronger now, so much more powerful. So much more distracting.

I felt the world tilt when the dragon became the most handsome man I've ever seen and started to speak to the wolf as if the animal would understand. When the wolf turned into a man, I stopped paying attention and began to go through the list of medicines I'd recently been offered for mental illnesses. I was going to need one for hallucinations, I knew that much, because this had to be pure hallucination.

It was my mother's doing, that's it! She'd planted the suggestion in my brain and now it had manifested before me as some warped reality. Or was this some game of hers? I cast a furtive glance but saw nothing at the house. Had she missed my initial scream somehow? How?

It was all playing out in a surreal play before me. Dragons and wolves turning into men, and just as I was fading into something I had to assume was a faint, my attacker turned back into a wolf and his snarling face was coming right at me, a paw extended to swipe at my legs. I kicked at the wolf, just as the dragon man landed on me in human form, and I screamed with fear and rage. Why was this one attacking me now?

I fought, I kicked, I punched, I scratched at him, but

all I accomplished was giving him my wrists as he straddled my waist. I was panting, angry, my teeth bared, and I stared up into his beautiful face. Damn, how did one man end up so gorgeous? I thought in a split second before anger returned. That didn't stop my body from reacting to him in a most embarrassing way. I felt a moan bubbling in my throat as he leaned over me, his nose coming close to my face as he inhaled my scent.

"A huntress, are you? Fuck me!" He'd whispered the words, his eyes hot and burning into mine. "Mary, get rid of those three. I'll be back later to give my report to father." Mary grunted behind him, and the others shifted, taking the wolves with them as they flew away.

"Huntress? I take it my mother put you up to this?" I struggled against the iron vice that was his one fist holding my hands above my head. I felt vulnerable, but still safe. Safe enough that I felt my nipples respond to the way my breasts were pushed up against his chest as he inhaled my scent once more.

"Hush woman, I don't want the others to hear. I don't know who your mother is but I do know you are a dragon hunter, mate."

I had to assume that mate part was a leftover from the English accent he spoke with. The dragon hunter part? That was all my mother. I was so angry I could kick him right in the wobbly bits!

"Get off me, you idiot. Dragon hunter, my ass. Get

the fuck off me!" I pushed at his chest and he flew away from me, his face a mask of shock as power surged through my arm and out to him.

"Mate, indeed." He didn't look happy as he said it. "You don't know what you are, who you are?"

"If you're talking about that crazy shit my mom keeps yammering on about then yeah, I do. If you think I believe it then no, I don't." I was swearing, not my normal pattern, but he seemed to bring it out in me.

I glared at him while I sat up and brushed my pajamas off. "Who are you, anyway? Some acolyte of my mother's? Has she got some kind of cult going on up here in hillbilly-land?"

He looked at me strangely, as if very confused about everything I'd just said, but he didn't look offended. Of course, he wasn't from the mountains, so maybe that last bit hadn't offended him.

"Your mother must be a dragon hunter too. You're part of the enclave, that's why you can see me. It's not just because you're my... Dammit!" He looked frustrated as he ran a hand through his hair, just long enough to give you something to grab on to when he was... well, that wasn't something I needed to think about right now, was it?

"Huh?" I couldn't think of anything else to say. He wasn't making any sense and it wasn't just because of that sweet accent he had.

I looked into gray eyes that shone like silver mirrors, wondering how even the moonlight didn't hurt those pale eyes. He really was something to behold, very tall, well over six feet tall, with not an ounce of fat on him. He was pure muscle dressed in black leather. I felt a quiver between my thighs and took a deep breath. Who *was* this man, and why did it feel like he'd cast a spell on me? One that made me forget the last few minutes and want nothing more than to pull him down to me in the pine needles and do naked things with him?

I heard a low growl from him as images flashed in my mind, and knew he was thinking the same. Alright, maybe we're both crazy. Maybe we're both going to end up in an asylum somewhere, but we could have some really fantastic sex first, right?

Down girl, I told myself, you don't even know… Oh hell, I don't care what his name is, I just want those full lips on my body, right now!

"My name is Malcolm," he whispered as he crawled over to me as though I'd pulled him with my eyes and my thoughts. Slowly, he eased his way up my body until our mouths were so close… only a breath apart. "And I am your mate."

"I…" I didn't finish because his lips were on mine and he tasted as delicious as I knew he would. I touched his face just as our lips met, and I felt desire burn through me so hot my nails dug into his cheek.

I moaned and opened my mouth and his tongue came inside, swiping at mine, as lost as I was in an instant. I felt energy coursing between us, into me, healing me, and my hips moved of their own will against him. He'd risen up between my thighs so intimately, and how he was pressed into me, *there*, so hot and so fucking hard.

"Malcolm," I whispered as he broke away to plant a wet kiss across my cheek before he slid down to my throat to inhale deeply. His teeth nipped at my neck, at that spot, oh God, that fucking spot, and I was his. I wanted to push my clothes away, I wanted to be his, I wanted him to be mine, I just wanted.

"What is this madness?" he whispered as he kissed a soothing path over the spot. "You are a dragon hunter and I am a dragon. This can't be. You can't be my mate."

"But… I'm just a human…" I forgot to finish because his hand cupped my breast through the soft cotton of my top, and his face moved down as if drawn to my flesh. His teeth nipped at the tight button beneath the soft fabric and my legs clasped around his waist.

"Please…" I begged him. Oh, I needed this, this life that he was surging into me, this wonderful ache that he'd aroused that seemed to have no end. "Touch me, please, make it stop."

I wanted the kind of rough and dirty sex I've only ever seen in movies, that kind with hot kisses, sweeping touches that made you squirm on your couch, and made you dream of knights that didn't exist anymore, if they ever did. I wanted to beg him to fuck me until I turned inside out and couldn't remember my name, and when he pulled his teeth away from my nipple and looked at me, I knew that was what he wanted too.

"Arista?" I heard my mother call and stilled.

He was gone in an instant, and for all I knew, he might not have ever existed.

"Mom? Who is Malcolm? You wouldn't happen to have his phone number, would you?" He was gone, shifted and flew away. I looked up at the stars, but saw no shapes in the sky, not like the last time I'd smelled that scent and seen a shape. It had been him then, if he was real.

I sat up and buried my head in my hands. This was just too much.

I heard her stepping through the twigs and waited for her on the ground.

"Malcolm? I have no idea who that is, honey. What are you doing out here anyway? Honey! Why are you on the ground, are you alright? Come inside, it's cold out here!" She gathered me up off the ground and we went back into the house.

She brushed at my chilled arms as she studied my face, taking me in with quizzical eyes. "What's happened?"

"I met a dragon and his wolf pals. Although he kept calling me his mate, so maybe they weren't all pals? Do you have any anti-psychotics lying around, Mom? I think I need one." I sat in a chair at the table in the corner of her kitchen and pulled the blanket she'd given me closer around my shoulders.

"I don't mess with that stuff baby, it clouds your brain too much. Now, did you say dragon?" Her dark eyebrow crooked as she sat down in the chair across from me, the kettle on to make a hot cup of herbal tea.

"Yep. A big ole black, dragon, Mom. A huge fu… uh, thing." I'd nearly sworn again. My mom wasn't a prude, but she didn't swear so I'd tried not to around her.

"And wolves? I'd heard there were werewolves too, and vampires, but thought those were just myths." She tapped a long fingernail on the table, her gaze inward as she thought. "I'll have to find your grandmother's book. Wait here."

She ran off then, her face lit with excitement. Maybe it was a mistake telling her. I leaned back in the chair, letting out a deep sigh. It wasn't my normal sigh of exhaustion though, it was only a sigh of weariness. What the hell was going on now?

I'd been attacked, twice, and just found out imaginary creatures were real. He'd felt real anyway. I could still taste his tongue on mine, the softness of his cheek under my palm, and the way his lips had given in to mine. I could still feel the heat he'd stirred between my thighs.

"Have you seen any rowan trees around lately, Arista?" My mother asked as she walked into the kitchen, her head in a very old looking book. It didn't even have a title on the cover, it was just some scraps of leather tied over a sheaf of very old looking paper.

It was a very humble looking book, but it also looked very old. "What's that, Mom?"

"Your grandmother's book. So, that's a no on the rowan? What about you? Or hemlock?"

I wanted to reach for the book as she sat back down, listing off more plants, but she still had her face buried in it, reading. I made the tea and set a cup on each side of the table. She didn't notice.

"I don't think we have any of these plants, my darling. How are we going to fight the dragons if we can't protect ourselves from them?" She looked as though she was on the verge of panicking, so I took her hand from the book and clutched it between mine.

"Mom, the dragons left. Without killing us. I don't think they're that concerned." I had to reassure her somehow. I knew I shouldn't have opened my mouth.

"But, neither of us has been properly prepared for them, Arista! Your grandmother was the last that went to England to train..." She had tears in her eyes, and I squeezed her hand.

"Grams went to England? I didn't know that." I didn't know a lot about the woman, really.

"She did, during the war. She ran off to join the Women's Airforce Service Pilots program, she was amongst the first women to fly for the Army, you know?" Mom looked at me over glasses she'd forgot to put on her face. She pushed them back down off her head in exasperation when she realized and grinned. "Yes, your grandmother wasn't just the toothless old woman you might remember from your younger days."

She had a gleam in her eye as she went on, remembering her mother. "She was taken to England to fly over there, just service missions, not the battles the men were going through, and while she was there she was given her dragon hunter training."

A thought niggled at the back of my brain. "Didn't they have to be pilots first?"

"Oh yes, but things were different in those days. Your grandmother used to do crop dusting with her father, so she'd been flying for ages by the time the WASPs came along. She was a stunner in her uniform too. Here, this is a picture of her in it." She dug through the book until she found a page with pictures sandwiched between the pages.

A smiling woman with both mine and my mother's face stared back at me, her lips black from the red lipstick in the black and white photo. She was lovely, smiling, and carefree. She looked far more confident than either my mother or I ever had. What a life she must have lived. A pilot during the war!

Mom was calm again, and her eyes had lost that haunted look, so I pushed her to go to bed. "Look, Mom, maybe that guy was just teasing me. Maybe he wasn't really a dragon."

"I suppose he could have heard some stories from someone in town. Still, somebody attacked you baby, and I won't have that. I'll call Anne tomorrow. We'll figure something out."

"Lord, just don't call Dad, alright? He'll flip his lid." I sat back in my chair again and sipped at the now cooling tea.

"No, you're right, he'll go insane if he hears about it. I guess maybe you're right. I need to go to bed. I'll do some reading before I sleep and see if there's anything we can do at all to protect us from those nasty things. They might have left but I bet they'll be coming back. They hate us, you know."

I walked out of the kitchen with her and paused at her door. "We'll figure something out tomorrow, alright Mom? Don't worry about it tonight."

"Honey, for most of my life, people have looked at me with pity in their eyes. Even you have since you've been back. I know something good has happened because your health has improved. You have color in your cheeks again and your eyes aren't so hollowed out."

She stopped, her finger tracing my cheek as she looked at me sadly. "You aren't looking at me like that now. Something's changed. So either we're both crazy now, or I've always been right. If I'm right, then we could be in danger. I won't sleep until I know I can keep you safe. You're my baby and I just got you back. I don't want to lose you again."

"You won't, Mom. I don't think you have to worry." I cupped her hand against my face and kissed her palm. "I'm sorry, Mom. I love you."

"It's okay, baby. Go get some sleep. I love you."

I left her with her book and her memories, but I didn't go to sleep. I couldn't, not with the memory of the way he'd groaned when he'd pressed his hips into me playing over and over in my mind.

7

MALCOLM

I flew over the coastline of America, the same word flashing in my mind over and over again. Fuckery. A shit-ton of fuckery. Bollocks and fuckery.

My mate was a dragon hunter? That was life doling out a serious amount of fuckery, and though I was grateful she was as hot as the sun, the fact that she was a dragon hunter was a seriously warped trick of fate. Perhaps I'd been watching too much television on the sly lately. It was impacting my vocabulary, and that just wouldn't do.

I huffed a sigh and saw smoke billowing from my snout. This just wasn't going to do. I should be heading home to explain to my father why there wasn't a tiny village in America mysteriously spontaneously combusting. Instead, I found I was heading back to the village, to her.

Arista.

I'd heard her mother calling her name out from my perch on the tree limb above her before they'd gone back into the house. She'd told her mother what had happened, but she didn't sound convinced that it all really happened. I suppose all our work to turn our reality into mythology had finally worked. The last remaining dragon hunters were now unaware of what they were, and that we actually existed.

That should be good news, and it would be if she wasn't my mate.

I could burn down her village and incinerate her with barely a qualm except for that fact. If I could actually bring myself to kill my mate, I would kill myself in the process. Without her, I'd wither away and die. Judging by how she'd quickly improved just from my nearness, I knew she was already feeling her strength return. It would take longer for me, but not that long now that I'd met her.

If we actually mated, then it would be even worse. A few days and we'd both be too ill to move. A week and she'd die. A month and I would.

So why was I flying back to her? Did I want to kill myself? Was that it? No, my body thrummed at me, you want her. You want to live within her, be in her.

I felt a shiver go down my long spine, all the way to the tip of my pointed, razor-sharp tail. I needed her. I'd never needed anybody before, not even my father.

I was at her window before I knew it, my body calling to hers.

It was something only mates could do, call to each other. I called to her now and she came to her window, a smile on her face. She'd been trying to sleep, but from the sight of her messy bed and messier hair, I knew she wasn't accomplishing that.

She'd had a taste of me, as I'd had a taste of her, and nothing would be the same. I pulled her to me, taking her lips in a deep kiss. She melted into me instantly, without a fight, so I pulled her through the open window to my body. Her sweet lips moved against mine and lit a fire in my belly, low and hot.

"Not here. We'll wake, Mom," she whispered to me when I let her up for air.

"Where then?" I asked, lost in this land.

"Where's your house?" She tilted her head, her fingers dancing along the belt around my pants just before she flattened her hand over my hard cock boldly.

"In England," I answered her with a hiss. That felt way too good. I placed a hand over hers, stopping the flexing of her fingers on my length. I didn't want to come in my pants like a schoolboy.

"Come on." I whipped her into my arms and shifted. I was thankful she didn't scream, I didn't want to deal with her mother. She clung to me, but my arms held her securely. She wouldn't fall. I flew to a city in an instant and landed. I went to rent a room in the hotel then came back to get her.

We could allow humans to see us when we wanted to, and our money was magical, or our plastic was, at least. Rich didn't begin to cover the wealth of my father and our family. Our cards were accepted anywhere we went, and this time it was no different. I took us down the stairs to the penthouse suite I'd rented, and we were soon in a magnificent room, decorated in creams and rich, dark browns.

We were on the twentieth floor, so our view was a panorama of the city below, but I only had eyes for the brown-eyed beauty before me. A bedside light lit the room softly, and I watched as the lines around her eyes began to fill out, and the gray color of her skin became healthy and pink once again.

My beautiful mate was coming back to life before me. Her body, too thin still, was softer, not so sharp, and her eyes became brighter with life. "You're astonishing, Arista."

Even her hair came back to life, a wave of a curl giving the light-brown mass volume. I buried my fingers in it and her head tilted back. Her lips smiled and parted just enough to tempt my eyes from hers. Red and full, those lips were made for me to nibble on. I slid my head down to hers, our lips coming together just right.

I moaned when her fingers dug into my waist, grasping at me for support as she gave a groan of her own. "Is this real?"

There was a quiver in her voice, and I pulled away from her.

"This is real, Arista, I'm real." I looked down into her eyes. She was tall for her kind, but not for mine. She was shorter than Mary, and it was nice the way she fit against my body as she threw herself against me.

"You'd say that if you weren't real or if you were. If I'm crazy and just hallucinating all of this. I guess I'm just going to have to be crazy, aren't I?"

"How can we prove this is real to you then?" I tried not to smile but couldn't help it. She sounded so adorable and I loved her southern accent. So different from what I was used to hearing at home or on the tele-vision programs I watched. I glanced at the bed, just feet away, but backed her up to the window instead. We were so high up nobody would see us, but I loved the idea of her bare back pressed into the glass as I fucked her. I wanted that.

"I don't know," she said as she slipped back, her head coming up against the pane of glass that made up the wall. "I tried to call my cousin to talk about it, she believes in all this dragon nonsense too, I think. She's sick so she didn't answer. I just don't know."

She wrapped her arms around my waist and held on tight and I knew she felt the pull of the mating. She glanced at me and I could see she was as helpless as I was. We had to touch, it wasn't a question of should we. She wouldn't be able to get enough of me, the same as I wouldn't be able to get enough of her.

Her hands began to move, exploring my body while I stayed still to let her. She murmured and praised my body, until my cheeks started to burn. I distracted her with another kiss. The only way to prove I was real was to make sure she felt me.

"If I'm not real, Arista, you wouldn't be able to feel my lips on yours." Her lips clung to mine as I broke away just enough to speak. "You wouldn't be able to feel my hands slipping down your pants."

Her shiver told me she was well aware of how real it felt, and she liked it.

"You wouldn't be able to..." I paused, slipping my hand further down, between her folds, into her slick heat. "You wouldn't feel my fingers sliding inside of you like this, with your walls clasping at me like that."

My own voice shook as I felt her surrounding my fingers deep inside her tight walls. My eyes closed as I savored the moment, that first touch, the whimper she gave as my fingers flexed inside of her. I wanted to taste her, but I waited. I wanted her panting before I got that far ahead of myself.

My lips moved down her neck, stopping when I found *that* scent, *her* scent, concentrated at her pulse. I nipped at the skin delicately before I licked it with the flat of my tongue. She shook in my arms, her fingers tensed at my waist still. I pulled one of her hands around between us, until she was cupping me.

"You wouldn't feel how hard I am for you, Arista. How badly I want this inside of you, surrounded by your wet pussy."

I could feel how tight she was as she pulsed around my fingers when I spoke, and I was the one with a tremble. She responded so quickly, so completely, and it was intoxicating.

I pulled away, just enough to push her top off, a flannel material that matched the bottoms with a blue female cartoon character all over it. I found it adorable, but when I bared her skin to my view, I stopped thinking about adorable. I stopped thinking at all.

Her breasts were just enough to fill my hands, with dark nipples that drew my eyes instantly. Such a dark, tempting color, and I wanted to taste them. I ran a finger from her collarbone down to the pointed tip. Her breath hitched as I made my progress, before it exhaled suddenly when I grasped the tight bud, squeezing slightly.

"Malcolm I…" Her words were a gasp, just a reaction, but I still answered.

"Yes, my darling?" I purred the words out just over her tear-shaped breast, my breath a feather against her skin. "What do you want?"

"I want…" She squirmed against me, her hips pressing into me suggestively, but I wanted to hear her speak.

"Tell me." I ran a finger to the other nipple, and she moaned.

"I want you, Malcolm."

"And you have me, princess. What more would you like?" I smiled against her skin when she gave a frustrated huff.

"I want you to touch me!" She got what she wanted then, and I took her left nipple in my mouth, teasing it with one hard suck before laving at it gently with my tongue.

"That's so good." She was purring again, and I pushed her pants away so she was totally naked. I don't think she realized just how vulnerable she was, how brave she was.

"Arista, you do know you're in a hotel room with a stranger, right? One that's about to fuck you until you can't stand up on your own?" I had my fingers inside of her again by the time I finished speaking, and she didn't miss a beat. Her hips danced against me, moving in time with my fingers plunging into her tight pussy.

She couldn't say anything, not when I'd found that spot inside of her that made her mine completely. She only writhed, her fingers grasping at my cock in one hand, at my bicep with the other. I watched her face melt into ecstasy and I inhaled her scent on my fingers. I held her nipple between my teeth, just tight enough for her to feel it.

She smelled sweet, like a drug I'd never be able to get enough of, and I swore I'd taste her before the night was out. In fact…

I sank to my knees, pressing her legs apart to settle there, my palms opening her folds to me. She was panting my name, her body perpetually in motion now, as my lips took her clit. Her fingers dove into my hair, and she directed me as she fucked herself with my face. I cupped her ass, tilting her into me, a better angle to give her exactly what she needed: my tongue.

She came apart against the glass, her lips whispering my name over and over again as I drank her juices. I was hard enough to crush diamonds, but I wanted her to come. She let go beautifully. Her gasps made my cock throb, her jerks made me hum in appreciation, and the taste of her that flooded my mouth made me hungry for more.

She'd been ill though, and rather than fucking straight into her as my cock demanded I do, I let her slide down into my arms and carried her to bed. She sighed sleepily, her eyes closed as I pulled the covers over her.

8

ARISTA

A dragon had just blown my mind. I settled into the luxurious bed, softer than any I'd ever been in, and sighed as my body hummed. I just wanted a minute to bask in the glory that was the orgasm he'd just given me. That was incredible.

I hadn't just come, I felt as if I'd just been turned inside out by my own body. He'd made me come in a way I didn't know was possible. Over and over that delicate little fluttering had turned into quivering pulses of 'oh my God'. I didn't know any of that was actually possible.

And it wasn't just because of the way he'd touched me. The way he'd spoken to me, the hums of satisfaction, that groan he let go of when he sank his fingers into me. It had all driven me into something I've never experienced before, not like that. I caught my breath while he ordered something from room service.

He came back to lie beside me and I ran my fingers down his chest, his shirt open to reveal the hard plane. Yeah, this dragon with the tanned skin of a god was real. There's no way I was imagining this. Hallucinations couldn't be this real, could they?

I inhaled his scent as I explored his smooth chest, a scent that intrigued me, and I sniffed. Before I knew it, I was sucking at the spot on his neck where it was strongest, and my hips were straddling his. My hand went down to grasp at his cock in his black leather pants. I fumbled at the belt before I found a row of buttons beneath. My fingers moved nimbly to pop the wooden buttons out of their holes, and then I had him hot, silky, and real in my hand.

I felt the throb as blood surged through his cock, and I wanted to taste him there too, but I couldn't pull myself away from his neck. He tasted so good.

He'd allowed me to explore him greedily, he'd let me become consumed with my own fire, lost in him, a madness that had overtaken me instantly, but he whispered soothingly now.

"Calm down, Arista. We have all the time in the world."

I glanced up, saw his smile, but couldn't calm down.

My heart was racing, my body was pulsing with my

need to touch him, to know him, and I wanted to know it all now. I stroked my hand down his cock and he didn't even try to stop me. I moved down between his thighs, and he pushed his pants away.

My fingers, eyes, and mouth explored him. First the tip, with my tongue, and my lips as my fingers stroked his shaft. His hips jerked up, pressing him deeper into my mouth. I wasn't new to this but wasn't used to a man so… large. He filled my mouth and I had to open widely to take more of him in. I'd never take the whole thing, not a dick that big.

I tried to please him though, and I knew I was when his hips began to move with my movements, a dance that only we could dance. He groaned as my fingers began a slick slide, the moisture from my mouth letting my hand glide over him. I sucked at the head of his cock at the same time, consumed with working him until he came.

His fingers wound into my hair, holding my head still and I knew he was close. I waited, wanted that pulse that would come with his first hot spurt, but he pulled at my head and moved. Pulling away from me, he flipped me onto my knees and pulled my hips up.

I was in heaven, on my hands and knees as my dragon took me from behind for the first time. I dug my fingers in the duvet and pushed back into him with a groan. The head of his thick length pressed into me until he spread me open with his hands. Then he was filling me, inch by inch, pressing me open slowly and it was the most pleasurable torture.

I could feel my clit throbbing in time with my nipples and moved a hand down to flick at the bud. I just wanted to come around him, on him. He chuckled and dug his fingers into my hips, holding me still as he slammed into me at last.

I was full, so full, full of Malcolm, and it was all I wanted. But rather than a quick fuck, he pulled out slowly. I felt every inch of him as he left, and I never wanted it to end, but I couldn't stop the urge—the need —to come. I was addicted to him from the first moment and I couldn't understand why, but I didn't care.

He slowed me down by setting a pace that had me in a near-meditative state, waiting for his entry, his exit, and re-entry. He pulled me up to grasp at my waist, to kiss me, and I craned my head to give him my lips. Again, he flipped me, and pulled my hands over my head. He held them there, and I grinned a daring grin.

"You like that?" he asked, and I shook my head, my hips moving in time with his as he sank back into me.

"I love it, Malcolm," I admitted, the tight hold made my breasts thrust up and down at his attention. I loved how wanton it made me feel.

"I have to admit, it makes your breasts look even more gorgeous, and I didn't think that was possible."

He bent down to flick at one with his tongue before he gave me a serious look. One more flip and I was over him, his cock deep inside of me.

"Use me, Arista. Make me yours." His eyes dared me to do just that.

I didn't know what he meant, but I thought I knew. I began to move, gently at first, until I knew how my body was going to adjust to his size. Then he started to talk in a language I shouldn't understand but did.

"I want to fill every part of you, Arista. I want to be inside your head, in your heart, I want you to be mine and me to be yours."

I looked into eyes turned into steel by his passion. They were now almost black as he became enthralled with my pussy moving on him. I rocked our bodies together, my pace picking up as he continued to speak.

"I'm going to fuck you every day of your life, woman. Fuck, look at you, you're gorgeous." I knew I was still too thin, but he loved me how I was. That's all that mattered.

I panted, the pleasure growing from a tight little ball between my thighs to a warmth that began to spread out as I rode my dragon. A dragon, he was a dragon! With a dragon's language.

I swallowed, emotion making my throat tight as I stared into his eyes, lost in him.

"I'm going to come inside you, every single time until

my baby is growing inside of you. Until you are so full of me, you give birth to a child that is a combination of us both. Perfect, just like you."

I felt my walls begin to clench around him and gasped in surprise. I hadn't expected to come again yet, though I was working towards it. I felt my hand twitching and grasped at his hands, hands I now had over his head. His tongue teased my nipple, then he sucked at it, which only made my clamping walls clench even harder.

"Come for me, baby," he groaned happily, his eyes drinking it all in as I moved on him.

I kept my hands over his, one on each side of his head as I moved, desperate for it to never end. Desperate to make the tension blow into so much more. I felt something odd just below my belly button, a swirling heat that snaked through my torso. It felt good, like he was touching me from inside, like his fingers were inside me, teasing at my nipples.

Having them both touched at the same time felt so amazing, and I thought that was it, until the flame licked down and took hold of my clit too. That's when I lost all control and felt my eyes roll back in my head. Everything exploded, my brain—my very being—as Malcolm's dragon pushed me over the edge and soared with me.

I was a part of him, he a part of me, and somewhere in the back of my head I heard a strangled shout as he pulsed within me, letting go at last. His body, my body, our very souls, were all mingled into one orgasmic being and we soared together.

I shook, my hands still tangled in his, my back arched to keep him within me, and we clutched at each other to hold on. Minutes passed, and all that could be heard was our breathing as we twisted together in passion, as we found each other and became tangled into one. He was mine and I was his.

That's how we wanted it.

I began to think the sensations would never end, that we'd created a new world for ourselves, but slowly we slipped back into our bodies, into our minds, and gasped for air as we looked at each other in shock.

"You felt that?" he asked me, his eyes searching mine.

"Yeah, I felt that." He was real, he was a dragon, and most of all, he was mine.

"That was the mating. My dragon came out for you. He wanted you too." He looked stunned. I guess he hadn't felt that before either.

"New for you too, huh?" I collapsed on him, my head on his shoulder.

"Yeah, it was amazing."

"You're real?" I said after a moment, my eyes closed as I listened to the strong beat of his heart.

"I'm as real as you are, Arista." He held me against him, stroking my back.

"Good, maybe I can convince my dad my mom isn't crazy now." I smiled happily, picturing the happy reunion of the two people I loved the most.

He stilled the soothing of his fingers down my back and went stiff.

"You can't tell them about me, Arista. You can't tell anyone."

I moved away to protest, and he stood up. A knock came, and he took the trolley left at the door by room service, hiding his body carefully behind the door. Food and champagne waited for us. I almost forgot what he'd said.

It played in my head as he set up the table with sandwiches and a decadent looking chocolate cake with mint ice cream in a bowl. How had he known that was my favorite? How could he know that and still tell me I couldn't tell my parents about him?

"Why can't I tell anyone about you?" I asked as I sat down, the sheet from the bed tucked around me.

"Two reasons." He put some potato salad on my plate with the sandwich and looked at me. "First, you're a dragon hunter. Your mother will want to kill me because I assume she is one too."

"I think I can talk her out of it, we have no idea how to even go about killing you!"

"Be that as it may, we still have problem two. My father wants me to kill you. And he's the king of our land, of all our land. You don't disobey him and live."

"What? Kill me? What the hell for?" I couldn't help but splutter as I put my sandwich down without even a single bite.

"You're the last enclave of huntresses to be found, you put all of our people in danger. I think our being mated might change that." He held a hand out to me and stroked my face for a moment. "You're getting better already."

"Is that your doing as well?" I asked. I felt amazingly better.

"It's not so much me as the by-product of our mating. You'll get ill every time we're apart from now on. So will I now."

I knew what he was thinking from the expression on his face: that probably should have been something he'd thought about harder, but he didn't regret completing our mating bond. I couldn't either after experiencing it.

"So you're saying if we aren't together, if we decide we hate each other and try to move on, we'll both get sick and die?" I found that a little hard to believe, but I had experienced it. My body felt better, and it wasn't just because he'd rocked my world. I *was* better.

"That has happened in the past, yes." He wouldn't look at me now, and I could understand why. This didn't happen, who'd ever thought up such a thing?

I knew it had to be true though. I wonder if that's what was wrong with Willow too?

"You know, my cousin has the same exact illness as me. We got sick around the same time too…" I let my words trail off, wondering if he'd come to the same conclusion.

"You think she has a shifter mate as well?"

Ah, I knew he was a smart man! "I do have to wonder. It's this same kind of wasting sickness, the doctors couldn't explain it for either of us."

"She's your cousin on your mother's side?" he asked me with a quirked eyebrow. That made my heart flutter a bit, that intense gaze directly on me.

"Yes. What if that's what's wrong with her?" I looked down at my hands, then at the sandwich I couldn't eat now. Everything had suddenly become too real for me.

"Then we have to find her mate." He took my hand. "Give it all time to sink in, Arista. This is a lot to take in, and you're only going to get more shocks as time goes on, believe me. Especially when you see my world."

"I know, but Willow… she's so sick right now. We have to find her mate." I looked back up at him and saw understanding there.

"If it is your desire, we will try. I just don't know where to begin." He did look lost for a moment, and I felt bad for him.

"Maybe, since you found me, he'll find her." I could hope anyway.

I knew I was running out of time before Malcolm showed up, I knew Willow was too. I could only hope we found her mate in time.

"How do we handle that then? If I can't tell anyone about you, I mean? How do I tell Willow what's wrong with her?"

"Maybe you should wait until we find the mate. We don't want to give her false hope."

"You're right about that. Damn, this is complicated." I took a bite of my sandwich at last. I didn't want to waste it. Not when I knew it would do me good now.

"It is, but we'll get through it somehow. I just have to find a way to convince my father to call off his death orders."

I stared at him, the sandwich now as dry as sawdust in my mouth. I'd tried to forget that part, but he'd brought me right back to reality. What the hell were we going to do?

9

MALCOLM

I cut through the clouds, my wings splayed and absorbing the heat of the sun. I didn't mind my human form, and I preferred it around others, but my dragon loved to be free of the confines of the human cage. I felt free in this shape, and one with nature. It didn't hurt that I could fly faster than anything invented by humans, and it didn't cost me a thing but energy.

I was circling the ocean, trying to make a decision. It wasn't an easy decision to make either. Continue to defy my father's orders or reveal everything to him. I sometimes felt as if my soul was breaking in two, but when I was with Arista, I was whole again.

Arista.

Thoughts of her danced in my head as I flew through the clouds, moisture beading on my dragon face pleasantly. For a week now, I'd been visiting her in the dark hours, taking her to hotels and cabins lost deep in the woods. I had a problem, though, a wolf problem.

The wolf that attacked her knew she was a hunter.

"Why are you protecting the dragon slayer, dragon?" he'd asked me when I went in to question him the first day we'd had him in custody.

"She's not a hunter, you're imagining things." I'd hoped my warning look would shut him up, but the sly man with the knowing eyes only grinned further.

"Don't tell me you have a thing for the slayer, dragon? How can that be possible?" He'd been resting on the narrow bed in his dank prison cell, a throwback to medieval times, shackle around his ankle and all. I'd buried him in the oldest part of our underground prison, hoping none of the others of our security force would find him to question him.

"Look, she's not a hunter or a slayer as you insist on calling her. She's just a human, got it?" I stared at him, my eyes changing as the dragon threatened to come out of me.

He shrank back, his bravado gone suddenly. "Fine, dragon. You'd better hope nobody else finds me down here or I'll tell them how you aren't doing your duty."

"It might buy you your freedom, but that freedom won't last long if you do, wolf. I will hunt you down and turn you into ashes." I knew he understood by the way he pulled his legs up and suddenly lost all signs of defiance.

The threat of not existing seemed to do the trick finally, but how long would that last? I'd taken the wolf his meals, cleaned his cell, and attended to his needs myself, all to keep the others from going anywhere near him.

My father could not know about Arista. My brothers and sister thought she was just a human woman the wolf had attacked. How they hadn't sensed her dragon hunter status I didn't know, but they hadn't. I wanted to keep my mate off their radar as long as possible.

If father knew about her, he'd order me to kill her. So far, I'd managed to keep him happy by telling him the hunters were elusive and that I'd been unable to trace them. An uprising in the wolf world when their leader was taken prisoner and vanished kept my siblings busy so far, but I didn't know how long that would last either.

I was in a mess of epic proportions and had no idea what to do about it. As the eldest, I normally held the answers to the problems, I was the one that took charge. In this instance, I didn't know what to do. If Arista had not been my mate, I'd have followed my father's orders, I'd have wiped out her entire clan, but she was my mate.

I could be ruthless, yes, but not with her. I couldn't bring her to my world either. She had instincts, powers that she didn't realize she had. Her strength, far superior to any other humans, was a sign of her status as a hunter. If I brought her to my world, her other instincts would kick in. I had to assume that she hadn't killed me, or attempted to, because we were mates.

What would happen if I brought her to a world filled with dragons? Would she go mad and kill us all, or make a very good attempt to? I couldn't chance her life, or the lives of my people on such a thing. No, it was best to keep her where she was, hidden away until I had to move her. I knew that time was coming, the wolf rebellion would be quashed within a day or two, then everyone would be looking for the slayers with me.

Father was already asking questions about why it was taking so long to find the hunters in such a remote area. I'd put him off, avoided him, and done everything in my power to hide her. I wasn't surprised to find that I'd flown where my thought took me, straight to Arista's house. I made myself as small as a crow and perched on a tree limb, letting the sunlight warm my leathery skin.

A squirrel screeched at me from its own perch two branches above me and I sent a little snort of smoke at it. The squirrel stamped its front paws at me and twittered some more. I squinted at it and gave it a little taste of flame. That sent it scampering off fast enough.

I didn't want the squirrel's tree permanently, I just wanted to sit and watch for Arista. She'd know I was here and she'd come out to find me eventually. I looked around at the forest and felt all the animals around me. Pine needles covered the forest floor, the leaves of maple trees and poplars protected wild mushrooms and other fungi from the sun. It was cool here, and the scent of the pine trees spiced the air.

I settled back onto the tree and waited with my dragon feet crossed. I could feel the dragon in me being soothed by having Arista so close. I closed my eyes and listened to the chirps of birds, the snort of a bear in the distance, and the voices of Arista and her mother in the distance. She would come soon enough.

I think I'd fallen asleep by the time she came. I startled and almost fell from the tree branch, catching myself before I did. I jumped down, in my human shape by the time I landed gracefully and stood. She had a wide grin on her face and I could see all of the lines that had aged her were gone now.

My presence healed her inside and out, and she was healthier than most people her age. Her aging process would slow down to match mine eventually, as mine would sync with hers, but we'd have a century or two to make sure she was never ill like that again.

"What are you doing here?" she asked me as she came near. She was in a pair of tight jeans and a black hoodie. The hoodie hid most of her, but those jeans looked as if they'd been painted on and sent my thoughts straight to what was inside of them.

"I couldn't stay away." I held my hand out to her, and she took it happily.

"I'm glad you came. It's so lonely in the day without you." I knew what she meant, the days were so hard without her near me. I guess that's why I'd flown here without even meaning to. I was drawn to her, she was a flame and I was the moth. Dragon. Whatever.

"Mom's questioning me, wanting to know why I'm better all of a sudden when Willow is only getting worse." She came into my arms when I held them open, worry creasing her brows. "I hate lying to her."

"I'm trying to figure a way out of this, my love. I just don't know yet." I pulled her deeper into the forest, to a dark place under the thick canopy of trees, a bower made just for us.

"I can't get enough of you. I can't think when you're gone, I spend all of my time remembering you." She spoke without condemnation or anger, only the truth.

"It's going to get messy if we don't find a way to keep our worlds from colliding." I pulled her down to a natural bed of pine needles and leaves.

"I don't want to talk anymore," she said as she followed me down, her lips finding mine as she strad-dled me. "I just want to feel you."

"We have to stop meeting like this." I laughed, but the fire was already rising in me.

"We have forever to talk, Malcolm. I need you inside

of me right now." She gave a low chuckle as she pulled at my uniform, opening the button-up shirt to reveal my bare chest.

Our skin put out enough heat to keep us both warm, so I didn't notice the chill to the air, even when her mouth left a wet trail down my neck. Her tongue flicked at a nipple and I hissed. Only she could make that feel good. I was hard and ready for her, but I knew she liked to be on top, so I left her to have her way with me.

Her nimble fingers pulled apart the laces on my pants and she soon had those off me, along with my boots. When she straddled me once again, her jeans and black hoodie were gone, and I drank in the sight of her tight nipples and supple body.

I couldn't help but close my eyes as she sank onto me in an instant, her need too fierce for foreplay. I'd get my chance to make her scream my name for hours tonight. For now, we were taking an illicit moment to love each other in the daylight.

"I can't get enough of you," she moaned as she took all of me deep inside of her heat.

I had no words, only a groan as her hips began to dance on me, shaking my thoughts away as she rode me. Wet heat, Arista's wet heat, was all I could focus on. My hands bit into her hips, holding her steady as she stroked us both in just the right way.

She was on fire, in a frenzy, as we moved together. "I

love how you ride me, Arista. How you take every bit of me you can, but I know that greedy little pussy of yours would take even more of me if you could."

I slid a hand between us, to the place where we were joined, and teased at her entry. She stilled as she looked down at me, a grin on her beautiful face. She bit her lip in concentration before she responded.

"What do you propose then, dragon?"

I hummed a deep sound of satisfaction at the way she growled dragon at me.

"I might be able to satisfy you, but you have to be brave." I gave her a mischievous grin and my finger danced away towards her other secret place.

"Oh, I see." She looked intrigued, but apprehensive.

"Come down here." I pulled her forward, my hand stroking at that forbidden place from the other side now. She shifted once again, angling her body so that her clit would grind into me as she moved, but also so she could kiss me.

Our lips met, and she began to move again, but I kept my fingers still, only teasing her for now. Sometimes it's the idea of something that thrills us, that makes our muscles go tight in anticipation and I knew that was probably the case for Arista. She wasn't a virgin but I wasn't sure she was ready for a full-on dragon session yet.

She groaned against my lips as her body started to

respond to my touch, to her rocking against me, and I knew she was close, very close.

All I had to do to set her off, was push just a little bit more, just a fraction of an inch on her tight little ass, and she'd go over the edge.

Arista began to pant, her thoughts flown, her concentration solely on what she was feeling inside of her own body, and I loved it. I loved how consumed she became with it all, how she gave herself up to me, to her body, completely.

My dragon came out and devilishly began to tickle her nipples, just as the tip of my finger stroked her ass, just as her walls clenched around my cock, and she exploded around me in a rushing moan of surrender. Her walls sucked at me, milked me, until I was right there with her, losing myself in the white-hot shower of pleasure that stole everything from me, even my name, as we became one roiling mass.

Her soul wound around mine and we were one again. This was why we couldn't get enough of each other, this was why we sought each other out, this mating that turned two into one, completely. One being without thought, without a name, only life.

I came back to earth with a crash as she gasped above me, her lips panting at my neck as she fought to catch her breath.

Maybe I could talk my father into seeing the sense of

letting her live. Of letting the others in her clan live too. I couldn't live without this woman, surely he would see that for what it was and let me be with her? I stroked her back as I considered this new thought.

I would go to him later and lay it all out for him. He'd have to see sense and call off the death order. I'd make sure of it.

10

ARISTA

I paced the length of my bedroom. An old sensation of gnawing need that would never be satisfied made me pace. I felt like a drug addict who'd been locked away from anything that might make the grinding ache go away. There was no substitute that could replace Malcolm, no drug that would make me better and I was afraid I was going to die.

Where was he? I clenched my fingernails, short but long enough to pierce my palms as I paced my small room. I looked out of the window, but my eyes saw what my brain already knew. It was dark, and Malcolm hadn't come again. I didn't sense him. I hadn't sensed him for days.

He'd left me that day after we made love under the trees and I hadn't seen him since. I chewed at my lip, not in a cute way that would draw the eyes of a man, but in that unmindful way, the way that would leave the flesh bruised and sore. The pain distracted me, but only for a second before the gnawing was back.

I wanted to roll around on the ground and scream for him, I wanted to search the world one step at a time if I had to, but I knew his world would not be found by human eyes, not unless one of the dragons took me to it.

I'd seen ghosts in the forests lately, the shades of settlers and natives that left this world long ago. I'm fairly certain I'd seen a vampire too—a pale creature with jade black eyes that had winked at me as I walked through the mall Mom had sent me to look for some special cream.

That brought my thoughts back round to her. She was trying to prepare some kind of anti-dragon cream and had sent me all over the area looking for a perfect base for the herbs she'd managed to order online. It couldn't be petroleum based, so we were having a hard time finding it. She came into my room just then and looked at me.

"You're going to have to tell me the truth at some point you know? You're getting ill again aren't you?" She looked at me intently, and I knew she was looking for the dark circles and lines that had plagued me only a couple of weeks ago.

"I'll be alright, Mom. I promise." I smiled a dismissive smile, hoping she'd take my words for the truth.

"I'm your mother, Arista. I know when something's wrong even if you were gone for years."

I didn't know what to say. I was thinking about telling her all of it, the whole truth, when my guts twisted, and I pushed around her to get to the bathroom to vomit. Mom, shocked, followed me in and soothed me through the whole ordeal with soft words of love. She even held my hair back for me and gave me a cold washcloth to wipe my face when it seemed to be over.

I was a blubbering mess of tears, snot, and other gross things when another round took over and I held onto the porcelain as my body tried to turn inside out from the stomach up. This time it was over with sooner, and Mom rinsed the cloth to wipe my face again while I rested my head on my arms.

"You are getting ill again, Arista. You didn't have this before, though, did you?" Her voice was soft, but there was a knowledge there that she wasn't sharing.

"Sometimes, but not this bad. I was able to control it for the most part. That was like being possessed. I couldn't stop it." I had stopped sobbing and took deep breaths through my mouth. My nose was still too plugged up to let me breathe.

"Rinse your mouth out and get to bed, baby. I'll put some soup on for you. Maybe you can keep that down." She helped me up and back to bed, her frail body a lie to just how strong she was. Like me, I guess.

I got my strength from her, after all.

Another week passed like that, and I wasn't even able to leave the bed for most of it. Mom cared for me, bringing buckets, towels, and whatever I needed to keep me warm, dry, and gross free. This was so much worse than what I'd had before.

Malcolm had warned me it would be, but I'd had no idea how right he was. Or that he'd leave me to my fate. I cried a lot, not just because of the physical misery, but because I didn't know what was wrong, why he hadn't come back. I knew he cared about me. I knew he felt our bond so I knew he hadn't just abandoned me.

Something had happened to keep him away, and I knew deep down that only death or his father could do that. His father was a king with a lot of power. Maybe he'd found out about us?

When Malcolm was coming to see me every day, it was possible to laugh off the threat his father posed. I knew he'd never let anything harm me, and I'd felt safe. Now, I jumped at every shadow. I screeched one night when a ghostly woman came into my room, moaning and waving her arms at me. She frightened the life out of me, with her all-white appearance and wide staring eyes.

Her mouth was just a wide hole that could not form words, only moans. Mom had come rushing in and shooed the woman away.

"I don't know why they've chosen now to bother you." Mom was exasperated and closed the curtains I'd left open to keep an eye out for wandering shifters out to do us harm.

I don't know why I'd done that, I barely had the strength to leave the bed, much less fight off a magical being. I hadn't been able to even ward off a ghost, for heaven's sake!

"Fu…um, well." I felt my cheeks flame, I'd been about to swear again.

"You and your bad words. I'll never understand the fascination." Mom glanced over the room, pulled my covers back up from the foot of the bed where I'd kicked them, and checked the temperature of the ginger ale she'd left for me earlier. There was still ice in it, so she left it alone.

"I guess you won't be going back to Atlanta for a while." Mom broached the subject we hadn't discussed since I'd mentioned it a week ago.

I'd been considering going back home, to have my own place back so Malcolm wouldn't have to keep taking me to hotels, though I did love the luxury. Now I could barely make it to the bathroom on my own.

"No, I suppose I won't."

"Your dad still at his cousin's place?" She was folding up some clothes she'd brought in earlier and left in a basket, not looking at me.

"As far as I know. He was supposed to come and get me tonight for dinner, but I don't think I'll make it out of bed."

"Do you think… no, probably not." She'd glanced back at me, a smile on her face before another thought wiped it away.

"What, Mom?" I knew she still loved Dad. Getting them back together was a goal I wasn't sure how to attain.

She loved him, even after he'd hurt her so badly. And he loved her, I could see it when he came around. He'd stopped getting out of the car when he came to pick me up, but he'd always look for her, and it would take him a long minute to start the car when I got in. He'd take that minute to watch her, his eyes tellingly wet, before he'd swipe at his face and put the car in reverse.

"Nothing, honey. I guess it's too late for things like that. Anyway, Anne's coming over in the morning, she's helping to bring Willow over. We thought it might cheer you both up a bit."

She'd sidestepped the discussion about Dad like an expert, and I knew I got that technique from her. I felt a smile stretch my tired face before I rolled over into the covers. I had a feeling the nausea would be back soon enough and wanted to rest while I could.

"Get some sleep, baby. I'll be in my room if you need me." She kissed my forehead and turned the light off.

Dreams plagued me throughout the night, and I woke up the next day feeling as if I hadn't slept at all. Willow walked in, though she did it slowly, and climbed into the bed with me. As though time and distance hadn't separated us, we twined together, two little girls seeking comfort in each other.

"I'm so glad you came," I whispered to her, as the older ladies chatted in the kitchen. "I don't feel so alone now."

Her arms were around my waist, her head on my shoulder, and it felt right. Comforting and safe, like home is supposed to feel.

"I can always breathe better around you." She sighed happily, and I wanted to save her so much it hurt. I had no idea how to find her mate.

"It's all that vapor rub Mom has in the room. I think she's boiling it in a pot in the kitchen too."

She tried to laugh but it turned into a cough that shook her.

She rolled off me and onto the pillow beside mine. Her eyes, so similar to my own, looked hollow and dark. I pushed her hair out of her face, remembering the girl she'd been. She looked like she was in her late forties now, far too old for the young woman beneath all of that sallow skin.

"What are we going to do, Will?" I asked, hoping she

might have a family secret stashed away. I knew she didn't or she'd have used it on both of us.

"You remember how we saved those kittens that time, Ris? The ones somebody had thrown out of a truck by your mom's house? I wish somebody would come pick us up and save us like we did those kittens."

Her voice was tired, her accent even thicker with exhaustion. Mine probably wasn't much better.

"I remember how we gave them all new homes, but it took weeks to make them healthy enough to give away. You reckon we'll take as much work?" I was trying to make her smile but knew it wasn't a very good joke.

"I think all the doctoring in the world couldn't save us now, Ris. I think…" She paused, her eyes going to the door. "I think I'm about done."

"Don't give up, Will! You can't! I'll be alone then!" I searched for her hand under the covers and found it. I brought it to my face and stroked my cheek with our joined hands. "You're my favorite cousin. I need you."

"I won't, Ris, I'm just tired. I'm always tired." She tried to roll over but the covers were too heavy for her. I lifted them, and she moved onto her back. "Thanks."

"I remember those slumber parties we had too. Maybe you can stay the night tonight? We'll watch movies on my laptop and Mom will feed us from that bottomless pot of soup she has, and we can pretend we're girls again, without a care in the world."

"I'd like that." She looked over at me, her eyes, just a shade lighter than mine, shining with happiness. "I know you're just trying to distract me, though."

"I might be, but it's better than what I've been doing on my own. Mom keeps going on about this dragon stuff and I've done some research. It's all myths and fiction, even that stuff from a long time ago when they were supposed to be real. There's not a shred of evidence they ever really existed."

"That might be, but I think we're both sick for a reason. I think it's something to do with that dragon stuff."

"Why do you think that?" I tensed then forced myself to relax. What did she know?

"Well, maybe we're sick because we haven't killed any dragons," she started, but soon stopped. "But then, why aren't our mothers sick, or any of the other women in the clan?"

"There aren't many of us left. Maybe we're the last and our dragon huntress abilities are doing something weird to us." I was trying to throw her off, but that sounded weak even to me.

"I don't know, it was just an idea I had. It's something to do with this dragon business, but I don't know what. I don't even think there are any dragons left, anyway. And aren't all the great dragons slayed by men? I never heard a legend about a female dragon slayer!"

"That's because the men in those days couldn't admit a woman saved them, Will," my mother said as she came in with two bowls of oatmeal and some toast, enough for both of us.

"Ah, that's it, the old male chauvinism trick, eh?" I teased, sitting up and helping Willow do the same.

"Gets us every time," Mom said with a laugh. She put the tray down over my lap and Anne brought in two glasses of orange juice.

"Hey Anne, how are you?" I asked the older lady. She was big with broad shoulders, and her smile was a pure delight.

"I'm better than you, sprite. A lot better than you. Eat up, I just wanted to see if you wanted something special from town?"

"Chocolate. And popcorn. What else, Will?" I glanced over at my cousin, hoping she'd join the festive mood.

"Guacamole and tacos! And some jalapenos!" She paused as she thought, a grin making her face bright again. "You know what? Some of those nachos and cheese from your store would be sublime!"

"Oh, that crap will kill you, Willow! I only put that machine in for the likes of Jerry Prater and his bunch!"

"It might be crap, Anne, but it's glorious crap!" Willow's smile did not dim, and I knew the movie night idea was a good one. It would lift our spirits anyway.

"Well, if that's what you want!" She sounded like she

was angry, but I knew she was pleased to see us both smiling. "I'll bring you a whole bucket of both later."

She left then and Willow and I giggled, kids again as we plotted out what to watch first. We might be dying, but we're going to go down with a bucket list of films checked off, we decided.

Now, if I could just figure out a way to find Malcolm as easily as I'd found a way to make my cousin smile, life would be perfect. I knew that wasn't going to happen, and decided to make the best of what time I had left. Something had happened to my dragon or he'd be here by my side. I knew that for a fact.

11

MALCOLM

My dragon raged. I raged. But nothing could break the silver lining of the cell that contained me. It wasn't even a strong silver lining, just a thin sheet, less than a hairsbreadth, but it was enough to keep me from touching the bars or the walls around me.

Silver wasn't just used to control werewolves, it could be used to control any kind of shifter. Our skin would burn if we touched even a small amount of it. The floor, my bathroom area, and my bed were the only part of the cell that didn't have silver over it. I wanted to scream in frustration that I couldn't break down the walls.

He'd chosen well, knowing I'd risk death to get back to Arista. Even I wouldn't touch the silver, though. The metal had a way of sinking into your skin. Tiny, microscopic pieces would invade a dragon body, tear through it, burning far more than the part we touched. It meant death to touch it without a barrier.

I could use my clothes, or my blanket, but the walls here were thick, and I was underground, I'd never get through it all before I died.

My father had imprisoned me and the sickness was tearing away my strength already. I had tried to reason with him, but he wouldn't hear a rational argument when he found out his son was mated to a hunter. He'd ordered me thrown into a prison cell and screamed for a historian as I was dragged away. He was trying to find a way to break the mating but I knew he wouldn't find anything. Nobody ever had.

I stared at the shiny walls glumly. Pain gnawed at my stomach, and weakness nearly stole my breath as it flowed through me in waves that only grew stronger every day. I knew Arista would be ill, much worse than me by now. That was the part that hurt the most, knowing that for all of my complaints right now, hers were far worse. My mate was dying and there was nothing I could do to stop it!

I hadn't reached the point of screaming in madness yet, but I was close. What should have been a logical, simple discussion between father and son had turned into a nightmare. My father had flipped over his writing table—a thick, ornate piece of mahogany that he'd had for centuries—turning it into splinters when I revealed my deception.

The odd part was, he wasn't angry that I'd betrayed him and our kind, it was that fate had decided my mate was a hunter that had totally enraged him. I think even he understood what the mating could do to a soul. I hoped he did anyway.

I'd tried to send him messages, begging him to let me out to go to her, but he hadn't responded. I didn't know how Arista was but I knew she was still alive. I could feel her in my soul, and even though she was growing weak, I knew she was still alive. I could only eat, pace, and breathe, hoping Father would soon see sense.

I hadn't seen anyone but my guard since I'd been brought here. There wasn't anyone I could plead my case to or beg to help me. Not even my siblings had come, and that stung. Perhaps Father had ordered them not to.

There was nothing to distract me from my own thoughts, and soon I was staring at the floor again. I could tunnel down, though it might take me centuries. I imagined this weakness must be how humans felt, this lack of strength and speed. What a miserable life. Even Arista in her healthy state had more strength than I did in that moment.

I heard the jangle of keys and stopped pacing. I stood well away from the door. I didn't want to give them a reason to attack me, not when I was already so weak. I wouldn't win a battle between myself and a guard at this point. I suspected they knew it too.

"Stand back, prisoner." You lost all sense of identity when you became a prisoner. Your name was never spoken, you weren't allowed to write it, and it would not appear on any documents. You would be prisoner in cell number. In my case, cell 277.

"You may leave us." My father, regal in his stature and bearing, joined me in my cell. That was the last thing I'd expected.

The guard closed the cell door and left, and my father stared at me. "You don't appear to be well, Malcolm."

"What did you expect, Father? A full-on greeting party?" I sneered the words at him, the first time in my life I'd ever done so.

I'd always looked up to him, but now I just wanted to throw him to the side and escape to Arista.

"Your uncle died at the hands of the hunters, Malcolm, or have you forgotten?" His tone was imperious, cold, and detached, unlike the fatherly adoration I'd grown up hearing. He sounded rather like he was talking to a wayward student, one in need of a good talking to and perhaps a hiding, but definitely a good dressing down.

I stared at the circlet of gold on his head, not giving him the pleasure of looking him in the eye.

"Yes, I know, Father. That was centuries ago. Lifetimes ago. They're dying out. We can let them die in peace and be free of them in the future." I'd tried to explain this before but I got the same dismissive wave of his hand.

"We can't be sure of that. Especially if you breed with this little hunter of yours." My eyes flicked to his. I hadn't considered that. "And what will happen to this unfortunate child? Will it hate itself? Will it hate you for giving it such an odd life, half hunter, half dragon? Heaven forbid!"

"I don't think it would work out like that, Father." I started to speak, to refute him, but he interrupted.

"Oh, I know the child would be a dragon, but you know *she* can't be turned, right? She won't be a dragon, won't become one of us as the wolves' mates do. She'll always only be a hunter."

His eyebrow raised imperiously and he looked down his nose at me. I wanted to knock the circlet from his head, but he was my father and my king. I would not assault him.

"I didn't think she could, Father, no. I just know she is not a hunter when she is with me. I think the gene is dying in them. She is not as strong as the hunter that killed your brother."

"Nevertheless, they must all be eradicated."

I stared at him, wondering how this was the same man I'd grown up with as a mentor. He sounded petulant, whiny, and not the same man. Could he be afraid of the hunters?

"Father, I will die without her." I tried to reiterate this point with him, but again, he waved me away.

"You will do no such thing. Godfrey is working on a solution now."

"You'd take her from me?" I was horrified. To have known the mating and have that ripped away? I'd never felt more alive, never felt so whole!

I didn't want it taken from me. I didn't want her to be taken from me. I knew in my bones that it was more than just the mating that drew me to Arista. It was her smile, her laughter, the way she sighed my name. It was how she made me laugh, how she made me feel. I didn't just want her because she was my mate, I wanted her because I loved her.

"I would destroy her with no compunction, Malcolm, if it keeps us all safe. I was going to let you out but I see now you'd just run to her. I can't allow that to happen. You'll have to stay here." He turned and called for the guard.

"I can't believe I used to look up to you!" I growled the words to his back, knowing there was nothing I could do to change his mind.

"You might do so again when you're free of this mating nonsense. Good day, Malcolm."

He left me then, his long leather cape scraping the floor as he went.

I looked down at my own prison garb, drab linen pants and a shirt that barely kept out the cold. I hated to think treasonous thoughts, but when a man would throw his own son into prison and leave him to rot, knowing he'd die without his mate, you couldn't help but do just that.

He would not get in my way. Somehow, I'd find a way to get out and get to Arista. Then I'd run to the ends of the earth with her if I had to. This would not stand.

I understood my father's anger; his brother's death had been what finally drove us out of the human world completely. Back then there'd been more hunters in the world. Now though, the handful in a small town on the other side of the world was not a threat. I'd seen how weak Arista was compared to her ancestors, and how she was totally untrained.

Even her instinctive skills wouldn't be enough to take down more than one dragon at a time, if they ever kicked in. I'd seen her that first night, I knew it was possible for her to have a natural battle skill, but I didn't think she'd become a murderous demon bent on killing us all. I knew she was different.

I crawled back to my cot and stared at the ceiling. If

father wasn't going to let me out, then I'd have to find a way out. Somehow.

Days passed, and then the days became weeks. My worry for Arista didn't help, and soon I wasn't able to eat. Life fled from me like rats fleeing a sinking ship, and soon I couldn't leave my bed. My hair turned white, I could see it in the mirror-like surface of the silver, and my face aged until I looked well beyond elderly and straight into ancient. Dark spots appeared all over my skin. I could feel my heart slowing down.

I went to my bed one day, and could not get back up when my food was brought in. The guard called for my father but I didn't see him. I slept, memories of Arista serving as my dreams, and I longed for her touch. That softness of her palm against my face, the comfort of her fingers on my back, was all I wanted. I was almost comatose by the time Father allowed Henry and Mary to come and see me. I couldn't speak. My skin hung from my bones, and my siblings could only stare at me in horror.

"What has Father done?" Henry spoke, his words an indictment. "I can't believe that's Malcolm!"

Mary didn't waste time expressing her horror. She came to me, her eyes full of tears that went unshed. Dragon's didn't cry.

"Where is she, Mal? Where can we find her?" Mary crouched at my side, her hand taking mine. My hands were still larger than hers, but now they were the frail, thin-skinned bones of an elderly man.

"North," I started to say, but my throat was too dry. She tilted a cup to my lips, and I sighed as it cooled the heat in my throat for a moment. "North Carolina." I looked up at her, pleading with the last of my strength, "Bring her to me."

"Right, we'll need to keep this quiet," Henry said. "If anybody outside of our family knows there's a hunter in their midst…"

His words trailed off as blackness took me. I just wanted to hold Arista one more time before I died. That was all. I wanted to hold my mate once more. I knew I was too far gone to be saved now, there was nothing they could do to bring me back.

Father had killed me with his merciless hatred of the hunters, and there was no way to turn back time.

12

ARISTA

I laughed as the show Willow and I had chosen ended and glanced over to see my cousin was asleep. This was our fourth movie night, and I thought it might be our last. She was fading quickly now, and I tucked a cover around her to keep her warm. Her mother hadn't wanted to move her, but Willow had insisted.

She'd fallen asleep before the opening theme song of the show had finished, but I kept on watching. I was too worried to sleep and too frightened of the creatures outside to get out of bed. I'd improved slightly, despite how Malcolm hadn't come. I didn't understand it, but I wasn't as bad I was.

If only I could find a solution for Willow. She was so sweet and deserved a long life of love and happiness. I looked over at her and couldn't help but smile; even as ill as she was, she wanted to bring me comfort. She was truly a giving person.

I was doing better than her, and I supposed I could live in this state of stasis—caught between mortal illness and being fine—but I knew even that would become wearying over time. I was better, and for now, it would have to suffice. At least until I could find a way back to Malcolm.

If only I had some of these superpowers that were supposed to come with being a dragon hunter. I wasn't psychic and I didn't have the ability to blow flames at people or freeze them. I knew because I'd tried. Mom's old book had drawings of such things, but if I had these powers, how to activate them was a secret.

I slept after a while, Willow warm beside me. I dreamed of Malcolm, as always, but didn't find peace in it, only more longing. I rolled in the bed, restless and too warm. I woke up with a start, the last dream ending with a gunshot. I sat up and pushed my hair out of my face. I was glad I hadn't woken up Willow with my crazy dreams and decided to go get a fresh glass of ginger ale. The ice had melted in the old one and I could see the water sitting on top of it.

I was heading to the kitchen, glass in hand, when I heard a tapping at my window. I froze, frightened that it would be another ghost come to scare the daylights out of me but I listened to my intuition. There was a dragon out there, but it wasn't Malcolm.

I went to the window, hoping to hear some news of my mate, and saw a very somber, younger version of Malcolm. I realized this was one of his brothers, and he wasn't as similar as I'd first thought.

His hair was black where Mal's was blond, and his eyes were emerald green rather than steely gray. Their features were similar though, remarkably similar, and I grinned.

"Is he coming? Where is he?" I looked around but didn't see Malcolm. Willow stirred behind me and I turned pulling the curtain closed. She was waking up and I didn't want her to see my dragon's brother, so I climbed out of the window, nightgown and all, and joined him outside.

"Malcolm has sent for you, Arista." He didn't say anything more, he just stood there, his eyes steady on my bedroom window. What was that about?

"Fine, great, let's go." I was in a rush. It had been over two weeks, I wanted to see Malcolm desperately and this guy was just standing there, staring at my bedroom window as if he'd just found the best taco stand in the world!

"Who's in your bedroom?" he asked, turning to me.

"My cousin, and if you don't hurry she'll wake up, come on, let's go." I didn't even know his name but didn't care. Malcolm had sent for me.

"Very well." He didn't say anything else, he just shifted, and I climbed onto his back. It didn't occur to me to ask why Malcolm hadn't come, or why he'd sent his brother when he'd spent so much time trying to hide me from his world.

The dragon grew after I straddled his shoulders and began to climb into the sky. Before long, we were high in the clouds, but he protected me from the worst of the wind and cold with his wings and head. Malcolm had taken me through the nights like this many times, and I wasn't afraid of it anymore. I knew I had to stay still and wait, that soon enough, I'd be where I needed to be.

I wondered if there was a TSA and immigration in the magical world. Would Malcolm's father want a passport before I was allowed in? I had to assume that's where I was being taken because we'd crossed over the Atlantic.

Now that I'd had time to think about it, I did begin to wonder what was going on. Maybe Malcolm had been hurt and that's why he hadn't come himself. Perhaps he wasn't able to fly anymore, and he'd sent this rather stony brother in his place?

I decided I didn't care, I was going to see him soon

enough, and that was all that mattered. Before long, the sun was rising, and we were flying down to a coastal town that shone in the sunlight. We flew through some kind of bubble, a thin veil of something, and the world below changed. A castle surrounded by a moat, stood tall and sprawling on a hill with a village spread out below. The village was encircled by a tall stone wall and served as a barrier between the castle on the hill and the outer wall below.

A real-life castle with turrets and walkways for guards took up most of the space on the hill. It appeared to be three stories tall with flags jutting from the top of three spires. I couldn't help but smile as I looked the place over. It was every schoolgirl fantasy of a castle, where a young maiden would find her future king.

I wondered if I'd get a long gown with a corset to wear. One of those dreamy confections with overly long arms, a train, and a corset that would push my boobs up to my eyeballs. I glanced down and laughed, I didn't have enough of a chest to cinch up that high. I felt the most carefree and happy since I'd last seen Malcolm. He was near, I could feel him. It wouldn't be long now.

The dragon landed on a spot marked similarly to helicopter landing pad on one side of the castle, and I dismounted. He shifted right away and indicated I should follow him through a door. I wanted to stick my tongue out at the silent man but behaved myself as he led me down the stairs.

When he kept going, despite having gone down four flights of stairs, I started to protest. "Where are we going? Why is Malcolm down here?"

"Madam, Malcolm is a prisoner. As a dragon hunter you shouldn't even be here but this is a dire situation. Malcolm is the heir to my father's throne and he is dying. Now, if you'll shut up and let me take you to him, perhaps you can save him before it's too late."

"Too late?" I all but shrieked. "What do you mean too late?"

He was halfway down the next flight of steep stairs and I hurried to keep up. Malcolm was dying?

We finally came to a door that he didn't pass, and the man pushed it open for me. I walked in and saw two cells side-by-side, but only one with a door open. A tall older man stood in that one, a sour expression on his face. In the other, a man slept with a blanket thrown over his body. I felt pulled to that cell but the older man stopped me.

"In here, dragon hunter." His words were a smirk, a sneer, and I knew he didn't like me.

"Where are we?" I demanded to know. I could feel some instinct within me, primed and ready to attack this man.

"In my castle, of course, hunter. You can put away the hunter act, I know you haven't been trained. You probably couldn't kill a bug, as weak and untrained as you are."

He looked me up and down and I felt as if I'd failed some major inspection by the time he finished. "The hunters of old would be ashamed to see what their progeny have become. Look at you, puny, weak, and unprepared. I'm not sure why you worried me so much now."

"Who are you?" I knew who he had to be, but I couldn't believe it, even with that silly gold circlet with rubies on his head. I walked into the cell and looked up at him. He was taller than Malcolm, so my head had to tilt back even more than usual.

He looked at me with a sneer that set my hackles on edge. My fists clenched at my sides as I stared back at him, unafraid. Something told me I might be weak, but I could still kill this man if I wanted to.

"I am Godwin, King of Jorvik. You are Arista of the Carolinas, and my son's mate. You are my prisoner and will remain as such."

"Excuse me?" I cried out as he stepped around me and slammed the door shut.

"Malcolm will recover with you near. When he is well, and we have found a way to end this curse placed on him, you will be taken to the executioner. Have a good day."

He made to leave but I stopped him with a screech as I ran up to the bars, reaching for him through the irons. If I could just get my hands on him, I could snap his neck.

"Wait! What are you talking about? End the curse? The mating? And executioner? I don't think so buddy, I'm a US citizen, you can't lock me in here, and you certainly can't execute me!"

I heard an amused laugh from the other man before he turned around to face me. "Your citizenship has no meaning here, my dear. You are supposed to be dead but my son chose to spare your life. Here, you are nothing more than a tool, and you will be used as such. Good day."

This time my litany of questions didn't stop him, and I hurled some rather nasty swear words at him. You'd think that would have had him turning but it didn't, he just kept walking.

"Malcolm!" Stupidly, I realized he was in the cell right next to me a little late in the game. "Malcolm!"

I didn't hear a response, but I could feel him. I closed my eyes, listening, feeling, but all I could find was the faint sound of his heartbeat.

"Oh, Malcolm, what have they done to you?" My

strong fearsome dragon was only a shell now. There was hardly anything left of the man I loved.

"You must work hard, hunter, to bring my brother back from death. He's almost there now, so you'd best get to work." A young woman, another sibling I assumed from her looks, came out of the shadows around the guard's station and approached me.

Her hair was blond like Malcolm's, but her eyes were green. A gift from her mother, I assumed. Godwin's eyes were the same as Malcolm's: cold, steel gray. This female version of the man was just as beautiful as the male version was, even if her eyes were hard and full of distrust.

"What do I do?" I had no experience with this and didn't think there was much I could do when we were separated by a cell.

"I don't know, we've not had to do this in a long time, if ever. Not in my memory. Do what your instinct tells you to do." She didn't appear to be any more clued up than me. Great.

"My instincts tell me to crawl into bed with him," I told her, waiting for her to open the door.

"That won't be happening. Father won't allow it. Think of something else." Her eyes told me to hurry or she'd kill me before I ever saw the executioner.

"Let me think. Sheesh, I just got here, this is all really

way too much." My head swam, and I sank down to the bed.

Reality sank in then. I was a prisoner, as was Malcolm. I'd been kidnapped and my mate was dying. Oh, and his father wanted to kill me for being alive. Yeah, I think that was all of it.

I put my head in my hands and wanted to cry, but I knew Malcolm needed me. I pushed down the sob that was squeezing my throat closed and tried to think. How do you heal someone like this? Malcolm had said we only needed to be close to each other, but that didn't seem to be helping. His mere presence was enough to bring me back from the brink, which had been something I couldn't tell my mother all those times she asked why I was getting better again.

I didn't know why I had improved, but she'd kept looking at me like she knew. I realized I was stalling, distracted, and forced my thoughts back to Malcolm. I leaned against the wall and could feel his warmth even through the barrier.

"Can you move his bed to this wall? Bring him closer to me?" I looked up to see the woman still there. "I'm sorry, what is your name?"

"I'm Mary. The dragon that came to get you is Henry. Yes, let me get the key." She retrieved the key and went into Malcolm's cell.

I heard wood scraping on stone and a grunt as she

pushed Malcolm and the bed to the other wall. I heard some fabric tearing and then something banging into the wall before she came out of the cell once more.

"You don't have long, hunter. You'd better make this work." Her eyes, hard as glass, pinned me to my position on the bed. "I wasn't joking. I will kill you myself if you can't heal him quickly."

I gulped and put my hand back to the wall. I could feel him now, so close, but so far away. I could only try.

I pushed back the tears that threatened to spill from my eyes. Godwin was right, some hunter I was. I'd fallen right into the trap, traipsed into it happily even. I might have been stupid, but it *had* led me straight to the one person I wanted to see the most, so it wasn't completely pointless.

I focused my energy at the wall or tried to do so. How do you focus something when you don't know how? I imagined a purple ray of energy and beamed it at the wall where Malcolm was, hoping it would go through the cold stone. I didn't feel any changes, or hear anything, but I kept trying.

I didn't want to lose him, not when I'd just found him again. I put my hands to the wall and pushed, wanting to push through it to get to the man I loved. I wasn't just mated to Malcolm, I loved him. I couldn't let him die now, even if it meant I would die at the end of it all. I don't know what Godwin or Mary meant when they said they were trying to find a way to break the mating bond, but I knew what I thought it meant.

I didn't like the sound of it, but I knew Malcolm and I knew myself. We didn't need some mysterious quirk of fate to make us belong to each other. We simply did, mating bond or not. Love was our bond, not physiology. I just had to find a way to keep him physically alive otherwise we'd both die.

13

MALCOLM

I tried to open my eyes, but I could not tell if they were open. I tried to move, but I could not tell if my limbs had shifted. The world was dark and I wasn't even sure of my own name.

I felt as if I was on fire and there was nothing I could do to put out the flames. I didn't even know how to escape because I didn't know which way was up or which way was down. I could only hang there, in limbo. My mind was blank, no thoughts came, and I simply was.

I don't know how long I was in that place or even what I was. I just knew consciousness and unconsciousness, and those I could only separate by how much pain I felt. This was not a pleasant place. Time passed but I don't know how much. I could have been there for years or it could have just been days. Maybe only hours passed, but I didn't know.

At some point a light appeared. It was little more than a lightness in all the unbroken darkness. It began to glow brighter and was soon a real light. I reached for that light with my unseen hands, wanting out of this hell. This truly was limbo.

Thoughts began to return—memories of a woman. A dark-haired woman with eyes that made me smile. Her smile was even brighter than the light, and the memory of it made me want to find her. I had to find her. I didn't know why, but she was important and I had to get to her.

Between waking and the odd state of unconsciousness, I thought only of her. I thought perhaps it was her, that odd little light in the dark, pulling me back to the world where she existed. When I could I reached for her and tried to fight my way out of limbo. Time kept passing and I struggled for freedom. Each time I came back to the world of pain, the light patch in the darkness became brighter. I almost felt as though she was there with me, but I knew she wasn't.

I wondered who she was. My mother? My sister? A lover?

I didn't think she was a relative, not the way she made me feel. Well, the way her memory made me feel. The heat that seared my flesh began to leave me and my limbs awoke with pinpricks of pain. I knew I was coming back to life and excitement began to flood me. The excitement replaced the nothing that had been there before.

What would I find on the other side, I wondered? Would she be there, would there even be a world there, a world I was only starting to remember? I didn't know what I would find but I kept trying because I knew she was there, just out of reach.

That tiny spark, that little spot that was only just less dark than the rest, soon became an almost blinding light. I was close to escape, almost there. She was so near, I could almost hear her breathing. I could almost feel her next to me.

A new sound reached my ears over time. A sound of sickness that worried me. That worry drove me even harder to find her. I pushed against the state of unconsciousness that wanted to take me at every turn. I pushed it away from me because I knew she needed me.

Out of the darkness came a name. Her name. Arista.

That was the name of my mate, the name that meant the most to me. Arista.

I fought against the great weight that held my eyelids sealed, ignoring the pain that felt like my flesh was tearing, and finally opened my eyes to see a cell of silver. Memories rushed back, thoughts, words, and emotions. My father's anger surged into my mind, and even the memory of his cold stare made me shiver as I remembered the last time I'd opened my eyes.

I knew my mate was close, so tantalizingly close. Arista was very nearby, perhaps even right next to me. I moved from the bed, pushing myself up off the mattress covered in my stale sweat. My clothes clung to me. I knew I'd been ill, but that didn't matter right now.

Arista.

I was surprised I had the strength to stand much less move. Arista's presence, for I could feel her now, drove me up and I had to get to her. She had come for me in the darkness and saved me when nothing else could. I reached for the bars, ready to bend them open, but paused as I realize they were covered in silver. I was still in my father's prison, a prisoner unable to escape.

"Somebody let me out of here," I shouted into the small room that served as the guard's station. "Let me out!"

"I'm here, Malcolm." I heard her voice from a space unseen beside me. "I'm right here, my love."

I saw the nails of her fingers appear on the side of my cell, between the bars and moved to them, my lips brushing against her skin for a moment before I took her fingers in mine. I was careful to avoid the silver bars, but at last, Arista was here.

"You pulled me from the darkness," I whispered, my

strength ebbing as quickly as it had come. I sank down to the floor, her hand still in mine. "You came for me."

Gratitude and love flooded my veins as I felt her energy flow into me. I'd almost died, I'd been right there at death's door, and she'd pulled me back. That was the power of our bond, but more importantly, the power of our love. I had to get her out of this place, my brain screamed at me, I had to find a way to escape.

"I waited for you, Malcolm. I tried to think of ways to find you but I had no idea where to start. Your brother Henry came for me at last. I'm just glad I didn't get here too late." Her voice sounded strong, but her breathing wasn't right.

"What's wrong with you, Arista?" I let my head rest against the edge of my bed, nearly panting for my own breath. I was just so tired.

I didn't want to fall asleep again. Fear unlike any I had ever felt made me want to sew my eyes open so they would never close again. She was so near that I could touch her. I didn't want to lose her again.

"I'm... oh no, not again." Her fingers jerked from mine and I could hear her being sick in the cell next to me.

I heard her tears as she retched and I wanted to comfort her. I didn't know how to, not when I was unable to touch her, to brush her hair from her face or wipe away her tears.

"I'm so sick, Malcolm! I don't know what it is. I

thought it was the mating sickness but it hasn't stopped. It just keeps getting worse." I heard her pitiful voice, strident because of her tears, and felt a tearing in my guts.

"It's alright, darling, we'll figure it out. Calm down. Shhh. Come back to me, come on, over here, take my fingers again." Slowly, she pulled herself back to me, and I began to sing a song my mother had sung to me when I was ill as a child.

It was a dragon song, but I knew she understood. It was about the joy of flight and how it took away all that ailed you. Arista listened, her sobs going quiet as we held hands through the bars. I sang until I could barely sing anymore, and her breathing became even. She was asleep.

It came to me then, the reason for her illness. She was carrying my child.

I heard a small voice in my head. A tiny voice that laughed with excitement because he could talk to me at last. My child, our child!

"Father, we must escape this place. Mother is so ill and so very unhappy." The tiny voice of my son brought tears to my eyes, tears that I quickly swiped away.

"I will find a way, my son," I spoke back to him with my mind.

"Good, I don't like it here. They won't feed Mother

what I want to eat. I'm not quite sure what a taco is but when she thinks about them I want one."

I chuckled at my son's thoughts. Arista loved the crunchy little treats and I'd seen her eat many of them.

"They do look nice, son. Maybe we can make some for her once you're grown and old enough to help cook." I could picture our son in a kitchen, telling us off as he tried to make food for us.

I had to find a way out of here. That was all there was to it.

My mate slept in her cell, still unaware of the life growing inside of her. My son and I talked in the way of dragons. We made plans for the future and I knew that life could be completely different from what I had planned. I did not plan on a future with a child and a wife, but the moment I knew my son I knew what life I wanted.

Just then, my father came in and life took a new twist. He had ideas on how to free me from the bonds of my mating, he roared as he bounced through the door gleefully. He came into the guard's station, Henry and Mary with him, with a jaunty air that did not match his angry face. He gazed down at me on the floor and sneered.

"This is what you are reduced to for that dragon hunter of yours, Malcolm? Wallowing like a pig, in your own sweat and dirt? This is the life you choose?"

I glared up at my father from the floor, not recognizing the man before me. He had always been a fair ruler, but this was a hard man with an iron fist and I did not recognize him. Ruling a land of magic could be difficult but he had always managed it with aplomb. He walked a border between ruthlessness and vicious actions, but he had always been fair. I had never known my father to take an evil action, but it was almost as if he had gone insane. His eyes burned with anger, with glee at the pain he was about to cause, and I almost felt as if he hated me. The man before me had never been evil, but now I wondered.

"What would you like me to say, Father? That I will do your bidding and be a good boy? Because it's not going to happen. Breaking the mating bond will not end this and if you try it will not end well for you." I didn't care if the threat was empty, I had to make the promise, even with an uncertain future.

I could barely hold myself up against the edge of the bed, but I still held onto Arista's hand.

He looked at me and I knew what he was thinking. Hundreds of years spent keeping the peace between werewolves and vampires and between vampires and dragon shifters was in jeopardy because of me. That's what he saw at least. He had spent so much time keeping that peace that he couldn't break out of his own prejudices now. Where my father used to be able to find a fair option, he was now looking for the simple one that would tear my mate from my life.

The worst part was, he seemed to be enjoying it, and I just couldn't fathom why. Even if he thought humans were worse than the muck that gathered in the crevices of his shoes, this hatred he felt towards me was unreasonable.

"You might be the son that will take my place one day, Malcolm, but you won't take that place with this woman by your side." His jaw all but cracked as he spoke, and I knew he was furious.

"Father, she is my mate, and you can break that bond but you can't make me stop loving her. She is the woman I love and you can't break that no matter what you do."

"We'll see, Malcolm. You were always a good son, but you can't bring this filth into our land. She will destroy us all. You might not think it fair but breaking your bond is the only solution."

I didn't point out that he'd brought her here, not me. I was too tired to continue to argue. I let my head hang between my hands as I considered what to do. He was telling me that he was going to rip her from my life, a move he hoped would make me forget her.

I knew that breaking the bond would not make me stop loving her, if anything breaking the bond would only show me how much I truly did love her. My father would not understand. He thought the mating was the only bond between us. He was wrong, we loved each other, bond or no bond.

Arista was a true hunter, fierce and loyal, and would fight for anyone she loved. There was far more to my mate than just a shared bond.

"Father, you can try but the only way a bond has been broken throughout our history is through death. Try your best, you will not break it." I could cling to that hope. I didn't feel threatened by him at all now, other than in the matters of freedom.

I knew we didn't need the bond to love each other, Arista and I, so he could break it if he chose, it wouldn't change things.

He considered me for a moment, staring at me as he would a specimen in a jar.

"You'd better hope we find a way because the only way you're getting out of this prison cell is if that bond is broken. She will stay here forever if I have to keep her here, as will you, because I will not unleash her on our world."

I looked back at him, my world suddenly tilting on its side. From his rigid stance and the cold look in his eye I knew he meant every word he said. He would keep us locked up here for eternity if that's what it took. I could not allow that, but I didn't have any idea how to get us out of here.

I looked behind my father at my brother and my sister, but they were not looking at me. I—the man who was supposed to be king—was now a prisoner. Even worse, my mate was a prisoner with me in a world she did not understand.

14

ARISTA

I stared at the stone wall wondering if it would crumble if I stared at it long enough. I considered scratching at it, but I didn't think my nails would hold up to it. I could feel Malcolm through the wall; I could feel his heat and smell his scent, but I could not touch more than his fingers. I wanted to be wrapped in his arms, I wanted to see his smile, and I wanted to smell him all around me, but the wall separated us.

It had been days since I was brought here but I didn't know how many. There were no windows and no clocks to tell time with, so we could only imagine time passing. We spent many hours on the floor holding hands through the bars, talking about the things we would do when we were free again. My sickness was getting better but Malcolm did not want to talk about it.

I wasn't stupid. Well, I wasn't always the brightest light bulb in the pack, but I had an idea of what was happening, and why I was so sick. There was something growing inside of me, a child I suspected, but still he did not want to talk about it and he would distract me with thoughts of Paris or Greece, or even cold places like the steppes of Russia. When it was hot, a place like Siberia did not sound so bad. It wasn't hot in our cells and it wasn't cold, it just was. For some reason I always felt hot, and Malcolm would tell me about all of the cold places he'd been to.

I kept trying to talk to him about the suspected baby, but he found a way to distract me every time. Sometimes it was with talk of food, sometimes it was with books or films. We spent hours discussing our lives, the things we liked, the things we loved, anything to avoid talk of the baby and what our future held for us.

Sometimes the guards came and we'd go to sleep, so they couldn't hear our conversations. We truly learned about each other in the hours when we were alone. Malcolm had been raised to be a king but he'd never really wanted the throne. He wanted a quiet house on a quiet street with a fence that matched. He wanted a simple life with children and music and laughter.

We never actually discussed it, but we both avoided the topic of what would happen if we didn't get out of this prison. We avoided discussing what would happen if his father succeeded and found a way to break our bond. We just talked about the future that we both wanted. I would design my games and he wanted to design furniture. He liked the thought of carving something from a piece of wood and turning it into something you could use. We spent the days laughing away our fears and building our dreams for the future. We never once talked about escaping. I think we knew it was pointless, impossible without help.

We didn't see anyone other than the guards. They were the only visitors we had. I wondered if my parents would come but I knew they didn't have a clue where I was and even less chance of finding me. I missed my mother and father, but I was happy to be with Malcolm.

I had no idea how much time had passed but I didn't think it had been long. The baby hadn't grown that much. We just spent a lot of time talking and sleeping and walking around our cells for exercise. We were never allowed outside and we never saw sunshine, but it was okay because we were together. We made plans and I tried to come up with ideas for escape, but we were too far underground. That was a little nugget of information I'd gathered from Malcolm.

I hadn't realized how far down we'd come when Henry brought me here but now I knew just how far down we were. I felt as if we'd been buried, removed from the world and all that we knew, but Malcolm kept me sane. I'd never been claustrophobic but knowing there was tons of material over you could make anyone feel funny. Malcolm kept me calm, distracted me from the overwhelming panic by singing those strange songs to me from his childhood.

They soothed me and took away my fears. I wanted to escape for so many reasons, but at the same time being with Malcolm was all I wanted. I didn't want to give that up for the alternative; being ill and on the verge of death again.

"Arista, are you awake, darling?" I heard him call from his cell.

He'd been in the shower, a luxury for prison cells, I'm well aware, but they were only tiny and got water everywhere. I was just glad there was a toilet with some kind of privacy. I'd been daydreaming about the things we could do in a shower when his voice interrupted me.

"What is it, babe?" I called out from my bed, my hand now out of my pants.

"Could you stop being so horny all the time, it's driving me mad over here!" He sounded like he was trying not to laugh.

"I don't know what you're talking about!" I protested with shock. How could he know what I was thinking? "Is this one of those mating bond things?"

"You were having some of the naughtiest thoughts

I've ever come across, Arista! And yes, I guess it is. High emotions can transfer between us sometimes. Everybody's bond is different and for some it grows over time. In our case, it seems I can get some of your thoughts."

"Oh. So, you got all of that about me being on my knees then?" I felt my cheeks flaming as I spoke.

"Yes, indeed. And though it was a lovely vision, it was distracting when I was trying to get through the shower. You know the hot water only lasts five minutes." He was laughing now.

"Shit," I muttered to myself. Had he seen the bit about what I wanted him to do to me the next time we had a chance at sex?

"Yes, I saw that too. Now stop thinking about it!"

"I'm not sure I like this, Malcolm."

"You're the one that started it. Don't shoot the messenger just because you don't like the message."

"I'm not shooting the messenger I just don't think I like you digging around in my head," I said with a self-conscious laugh.

"Ah, but isn't it nice to know that soon you'll be experiencing the same thing?" Now he was just teasing me.

His voice was low, in that sexy kind of way that made my knees tremble. "Don't do that to me, Malcolm. You know I can't tear through this wall."

"But if you could darling, wouldn't it be nice?"

"It would, but we know it's not going to happen so stop teasing me."

He chuckled again and moved around his cell, getting exercise so his muscles wouldn't become weak. We might not be able to go outside but we could walk around our cells together. It wasn't the most romantic of settings, but at least he was there with me.

I tried not to think about those I'd left behind because it only made me sad. Malcolm's father was not going to let us out anytime soon. I felt guilty because I'd left my family behind, but I knew there wasn't much I could do about it. I imagined my mother was probably panicking, but I was a grown woman. Then I cringed because I knew that I had left Willow there to try to explain how I disappeared in the middle of the night.

It was thoughts like these that kept me from sleeping too often or for too long. The guilt would sometimes crush me and then I would start thinking about all the weight of the building on top of us and that's when Malcolm would start to sing. His voice was rich and soothing, and though it was sung in a tongue I didn't know, I still understood the words. The songs always calmed me down and dried my tears.

Or maybe it was just that Malcolm was singing to me, but I think it had something to do with the songs.

They were all about the life of dragons and being in their world.

"Malcolm?" I called out to him. "Where do you think we'll live?"

It was a game we played when we were trying to change the subject or just chase away some of the boredom. Being in a prison cell isn't always the most glorious thing in the world.

"I've heard Canada is nice," he said through the wall.

"Canada? I've never heard of anybody actually wanting to go to Canada."

"Lots of people like to go there, there are so many lakes and different places. A bit like your own country with its diverse terrain."

"I suppose so," I replied as I headed back to my bed from my walk. "It's not high on my list though."

I stared up at the ceiling, wondering how many more conversations like this we were going to have. There are only so many ways you could fill a day and we were running out. I wished for my tablet so I could at least work, but I didn't even know if something like that would work here. When Henry brought me, I didn't have time to look around for power poles or other sources of electricity, but it was a land of magic so maybe there was.

"Malcolm?" I called out again, my thoughts turning elsewhere.

"Yes, my love?" he called back.

"Can't you just magic us out of here?" I knew it was a silly question, he'd have done it already if he could do such a thing.

I was also breaking the unspoken rule that we didn't talk about escaping. I was restless and bored, a dangerous combination when it came to me. I don't cope well with having nothing to do. I sighed, waiting for his answer.

"You know I would if I could. I don't have that kind of magic, my dear," I heard him say through the wall and knew my question had disturbed him.

"I'm sorry, I shouldn't have asked." I rolled to face the wall, that nasty little wall that separated us, and pressed my hand to it.

"It's all right, Arista, I know you're only thinking out loud. You're doing well just to stay sane in here."

I felt tears welling in my eyes, followed by that awful sting in my nose I always got just before I started to cry, and tried to push it all down. Now was not the time to be emotional, but the tears kept trying to come until they were spilling out of my eyes.

I reached through the wall, at least mentally, until I could feel the heat of Malcolm near me. He began to sing once again, his voice resonating around the small room that made up our cells and the guard's room.

"It won't work this time," I sobbed out. "I'm just too

sad. This is a terrible place, and my mom must be freaking out. And poor Willow! I just left her there, she might not even be alive anymore, and here I am in a castle with my prince. Okay maybe we're in separate prison cells, but we're together and they have no idea where I am."

"We will make it right when we get out of here," Malcolm promised. "We will go to them straight away and explain everything."

"Depending on how we get out of here we might not be able to, but I appreciate you saying that."

"What do you mean?" he asked.

"Well, if we escape we might be running, and that's the first place they'd look. It wouldn't make much sense to go there then so we would have to go somewhere that they wouldn't look for us."

A noise came at the door then, the sound of the key turning in the lock, and we both went quiet. We never talked when the guards were here, but it wasn't time for the guards. Somebody else was coming to see us and I tensed because I knew that couldn't be a good thing. The door cracked, and I saw a boot appear. It was a small boot belonging to a woman. Mary.

"Hurry," she said to us. "We don't have much time. Father is away, and Alec is distracting the guards."

I ran to the door of my cell and waited for her to

open it. Malcolm did the same, and when Mary opened the doors we rushed together but we didn't waste time on reuniting. We just looked at her, waiting on directions.

"Follow me," she said, slightly out of breath. "Take these and fly away. Quickly now, before the guards come back."

I took two bags from Mary and we ran up the stairs behind her, my heart was pounding. I was waiting for a shout, a warning shot from a gun, anything that would halt our progress up those stairs. I knew at any moment we could be caught and now that freedom was so close I knew I would not go back into that prison cell. I would fight my way through an army of dragons to make sure we did not go back in those cells.

Malcolm took the lead and I ran with him, my hand in his as Mary trailed behind us. Freedom was so close, so close that I could see the light through a crack in the door. I thought it was the middle of the night, but the light told me it was still daylight outside.

It might have been easier to escape at night, but beggars can't be choosers, and we ran. Malcolm didn't even try the handle on the door, he pushed it open with his shoulder and the door exploded around him as we headed for the landing pad. He gathered me to him and jumped over the edge of the castle, but he didn't drop me. He shifted as we flew into the sky. We were free at last. I didn't know exactly how, and I wasn't expecting it, but one minute we were prisoners and now we weren't. We were flying away like the dragons in his songs.

15

MALCOLM

I flew through the day and into the night, following the directions on the map that Mary gave us. We had stopped to eat and to rest several times, but I knew we would be hunted so we didn't stop for long. Arista, my hunter, had become the hunted. I did not know the place on the map but I trusted my sister. She helped us escape when she didn't have to and for that, I would always be grateful. My siblings were always loyal to our father but we were also loyal to each other. I didn't think they would defy my father for me, but some part of me knew they would help.

Mary had suggested that Alec was helping as well and that was good as far as I was concerned. There'd been a note from Mary in one of the bags, a note that had been wrapped around a small vial. The note had said I was to drink the potion once we reached the new land. I would lose my powers as a dragon, but I would be untraceable. Anyone who knew me would not recognize me, which was an added bonus.

I flew south, and we arrived at our destination. It was a land of veiled women and men in long white robes or tunics with loose pants. This land had rejected the human world far more than we had. The houses were barely over two stories tall, made of wood, sand, and stucco, and were designed to keep out the heat. This was a land where the sun rarely set.

"This was a good choice, Father," I heard the voice of my unborn child say in my head.

I chuckled as I landed, shifting with Arista in my arms. "We can hope, son."

Arista looked around, her eyes wide as she looked at a scene that looked like it belonged in Biblical times. Donkeys brayed in busy streets of sand pressed so hard by wheels and feet that it was almost pavement. Some of the donkeys were pulling wagons, others carrying heavy loads, and men and women bartered in a market around us. Nobody batted so much as an eyelash at us as we moved through the streets, looking for a place to stop for the night.

Before long, we'd found a home for rent, two floors of course, with a nice courtyard, and ventilation that drew a nice breeze through the house. We spent the first week trying to figure out how to cook without electricity, how to wash clothes, and which were the best markets to go to. Arista got the hang of washing clothes while I figured out how to cook on an open flame and in a brick oven. We couldn't really store food and neither of us had clothes, so we spent a lot of time at the markets the first week we were there.

Arista loved the flowing dresses sold by the same women who had made them, and I learned to relax in the loose pants and tunics worn by the men here. I was used to tight leather constricting my movements, so it was nice to be able to move freely for a change. We spent most of our time the second week preparing her for a fight we knew would come.

I taught her how to defend herself, and saw her natural instincts coming out quickly. She moved gracefully and with purpose, her eyes always on the target. We practiced every single day, knowing that my father could appear at any moment. I didn't know if we would be able to withstand an attack but we were both preparing for it.

Each night the sun set for a few hours, and these we spent in bed, memorizing each other.

I was angry for the first few weeks. It was only Arista and her love that kept me from losing myself to my rage. I was angry at my father for wanting to break my bond with her, for wanting to kill my mate, and for putting us both in prison. I was angry at the world for saying I could not be with her because of what she was. Mostly, I was angry at fate for making us both what we are; a dragon and a dragon hunter.

When I touched her our son's voice would go quiet and he would retreat to his own place. it was then that I could lose myself in her and forget the rage inside me. She knew her body was changing but we still hadn't talked about our son yet. I was worried she would panic as she had in prison and I did not want to spoil this idyllic time.

As the child's mother, she should be able to hear him, but so far she hadn't. I decided not to worry about it because I knew we had time. I didn't know how much time we had, but we were making the best of it.

The bags my sister gave us were full of coins and food. The food was gone now but the coins would last us a lifetime. I knew Arista's fingers itched for technology, but she was coping well. Anything that was not a prison cell had to be better. She was already trying to learn the local language and often spent time at our neighbors' houses watching them cook. It really was a perfect time in our lives.

She came into the courtyard made private with high walls and palm trees, and fell onto the bed of pillows we'd made there.

"You'll never guess what I learned today?" she said

with a smile as she looked up at me, her beautiful face on my shoulder.

"What's that then, my love?" I brushed a damp curl of hair from her forehead and smiled at her.

"Donkeys are the only pack animals here because horses don't exist in this world!" She grinned at me, her eyes sparkling with laughter.

"That's a fairly good reason then." I felt her breasts pressing into me, and felt my pulse quicken. I always felt like that when she was near. I doubt I'd ever stop feeling that way.

"I also learned that women drink juice from a certain fruit to make themselves more attractive to the men. It's supposed to make them beautiful." She chewed at her lip as she looked at me with a speculative look. "Do you think I need some of that?"

"You know better, Arista." I pressed her back into the pillows, my body covering hers as my hand pushed the hem of her dress up. "I think you know perfectly well you don't need that at all."

She laughed, her head thrown back in total abandon. I loved her this way, free and relaxed, not always tense with worry as she'd been the first times we were together. Or scared and almost broken as she'd been in the prison. I think of all the things I'm angry about, I'm most angry at what my father had done to Arista, not to me, but to her.

This carefree spirit in my arms now was the woman I loved the most, and he'd almost destroyed her. I would not allow that again. I could only hope that potion would continue to hide me from my father.

I inhaled her scent from the pulse in her neck as my fingers teased up her smooth thigh. There were jinn here, and magical ways that were far different from my own land, so I had to assume the fact that Arista's body stayed smooth without the benefit of a razor was some magical trick the women here had shown her. Either way, I appreciated just how smooth she was as my fingers found her wet and ready for me.

"I have to taste you," I whispered in her ear before I moved down, pressing her thighs open as I slid past her breasts. The gown she wore, a dress of silky cotton and buttons, opened as I pulled myself down her waist, revealing her naked body to me. I gasped in air as I looked at her, always in awe of just how beautiful she was.

Her nipples were tight on her round breasts, breasts made rounder by her pregnancy, and I knew not to touch them yet. They'd been sensitive before she was pregnant, now she'd go off with just the right touch. I let my hands do the work tracing slow circles down her waist as I moved my face between her thighs. Teasing nips of my teeth on the inside of her thigh didn't shift that sexy smirk she wore, but it did make her eyes go dark.

"You ready for this, my love?" I asked her, daring her to say no.

"Well, I do have a—oh!" She gasped when my tongue swiped at her folds, folds I'd pressed open with my hands. Her clit was throbbing there, pink and ready for my tongue. "Fuck, that's so good. I do have a class when the shadows reach the well."

The only way we had of telling time here was by referring to the shadows on the communal well. I pressed my lips to her clit and hummed.

"Hmm, so you don't want to come on my tongue, is that what you're saying?" I teased her with another long swipe.

"Yes, I mean no. Fuck, just suck me, Malcolm!" Her fingers tightened in my hair as her hips danced up to press into my face.

She wanted it and I couldn't say no.

The part that really drove us now, was that we shared each other's thoughts at times of high emotions. Right now, my woman was at the height of her emotions, and her brain was full of beautiful dirty thoughts. They flashed through my mind as I sucked her hard clit into my mouth, flooding my brain with the most indecent thoughts. My cock was already a bulging ridge in my pants, but when her thoughts flooded into my brain I had to press myself into one of the pillows just for a moment of relief.

Her hands tangled in my hair, almost pulling it from the roots as the pleasure increased intensely. My own thoughts invaded her mind, filling her head with my own version of eroticism. She was bent over the table that we ate from in one scenario, up against the wall in a dark alley in another.

In all of my erotic thoughts about my mate, I was always inside of her, groaning her name into her neck as I filled her with my come. I only had thoughts for her, nobody else. She interrupted my thoughts now, when her fingers tightened just a little bit more in my hair. She was getting close and it was making me impossibly harder.

I glanced up to see her writhing on the pillows and felt the tight grip of her thighs over my ears. I searched in my head for just the right fantasy, and inspiration struck. I thought about her on her knees in that same dark alley, my dick in her mouth. Not because it turned me on, which it did of course, but because she loved it. She loved sucking my dick, she loved it even more when we might be caught.

"Harder, Malcolm, oh fuck, make me come baby, please make me come." Her begging only made my cock harder. I knew desire would twist her insides even after she'd come, but at least this way she got some relief from it.

I let her folds go, my mouth now tight on her clit, and sought out the entry to her wet heat. I was soon sliding a finger inside of her, and her walls clamped down around my finger. She was so close, so very close. All I had to do is stroke her in just the right way. I crooked my finger inside of her until I found that spot, that spot that made her stomach suck in as I stole her breath away in one fantastic orgasm.

Her hips surged down into the pillows as her ass squeezed tightly, and her spine arched her into a bow. That was it, that was the place she wanted to be. My tongue kept a steady pace as my lips gave her the added impact of suction, and she just kept right on going. I wasn't jealous, I knew my time would come and Arista would have me on my knees begging for the release that only she could give me.

I waited until her hips relaxed and her breathing changed before I pulled away one last time. She was done now, but I'd let her rest, no matter how hard my dick was for her.

"That never gets old. Or stops surprising me," she panted above me, her fingers now playing in my hair. I knew her eyes would be closed and she'd have a huge smile on her face without my having to look.

I knew her well enough to know exactly how to satisfy her now.

"Your turn," she said suddenly, and pushed me back on the pillows. I could only grin as her nimble body moved over me.

My shirt was soon in a palm tree, swaying with the fronds, and my pants were in the fountain, but I didn't care because Arista with her cheeky smile, had my dick in her hands and was wetting her lips in anticipation.

"I've waited for this all day." She breathed against my shaft, her lips making the long edge slick as she sucked her way down the length. "I've been thinking about the way your dick tastes, even when those old women were trying to tell me about how to get stains out of cotton. I still don't know because all I could think about was how you taste in my mouth."

With that last word, she took what she wanted. Her lips teased the head of my cock, sucking it until I thought my balls would explode in surrender, but then she moved down, taking me deep in her throat. She'd practiced until she figured it out and now she could take all of me.

It was a glorious sensation, but not as glorious as watching her do it. I loved the way her cheeks hollowed out as she sucked me, and I pushed her hair away from her face for a better view. I let her finish me that way, rather than taking her body, because it was what she wanted.

I didn't care what I might want, I lived to please Arista now, and I'd take control when she wanted me to. For now, I was more than happy to come in her hungry little mouth, my finger teasing at her lips as I did so. She swallowed every drop of ecstasy, and for now, life was completely perfect.

16

———

ARISTA

I came to expect the unexpected with Malcolm in my life. Over the last two months, I'd become complacent, and though I was always vigilant, I'd stopped jumping at shadows. Or jinn as the case sometimes was. So how was it that our day had gone from completely normal to completely insane?

We were now running through alleys, even through houses as we rushed to escape his father. Our day started out as always with breakfast, a bit of flirting, a lot of sex, and then lunch. Then Malcolm's brother Henry had appeared at our door. That's when things took a turn for the worse. Henry told us Malcolm's potion was wearing off and his father knew where we were. Worse than that, he was already on his way.

We dropped everything and ran, our hands clasped together as we ran for our lives.

We huddled between two buildings as we tried to stay quiet. Malcolm couldn't shift so we couldn't fly away.

I put my hand over my stomach protectively, the bulge of our child now more obvious.

"How are you? Are you alright?" Malcolm inspected me, his hands pushing my sweaty hair out of my face.

"I'm dying in this heat but I'll keep running. Any clue where we're going?" I looked at him, trust burning in my eyes.

"I think we should head to that place on the edge of the city. Maybe we can lose ourselves in that artificial jungle they built out there."

"Good idea. Sweaty times a million beats being locked up. Come on." I grabbed his hand and we were running again.

All I could hear was the strained sound of my own breathing, the pounding bang of my heart, and my feet slapping the ground in my primitive sandals. I hadn't even had time to tie my hair up before we'd left.

One minute the world was right, the next, we were running. We didn't even stop to greet Henry, we just ran, leaving him standing in what had been our home.

Now we had no money, no clothes, and no water, but we did have each other. The houses passed and grass began to appear the farther we ran. Soon, we were crouching in a tropical forest of greens and browns, our eyes searching for a place to hide. I struggled to catch my breath as we walked through the forest, but before long, my heart had stopped pounding and I didn't feel like I was going to suffocate anymore.

"Here, there's a cave here. Let me look inside first."

I leaned against a tree, keeping an eye out behind us but still thinking.

"Do you always have to be a smartass, Arista?" he called out with a laugh.

Oops, he'd read my thoughts again.

"I can't help it if I didn't see you magic up a flashlight. How are you going to look inside without one?" I smiled but kept my eyes on the path we came up when we made our mad dash up this hill.

The forest was made up of thick rubber trees. An animal trail had led Malcolm to the cave, and the hard-packed dirt hid our footprints, but I had to wonder if Godwin and his team would have the same thought as Malcolm did. There's something up there that keeps the animals trekking up it.

"Alright, I think it's safe," my king of the jungle called down.

With a grin, I ran back up the hill to the cave and walked in. The top was well over my head and the huge entrance was hidden by vines. I could hear splashing in the back and made my way to it. Water ran through the cracks in the rock back there, about fifteen feet behind the entrance. I cupped my hands to sniff it.

I'd sweated out gallons of water and needed to replace it. The baby was kicking around in my tummy in protest already, so I knew I needed water.

"It's safe, I think. I'd be happier if we could boil it, but we don't have a way to do that." Malcolm came up beside me to have his own drink.

A rumble of thunder shook the walls of the cave, and we both looked behind us. The sky had been clear when we first came in, only moments before. A storm was coming, and we didn't have long by the sound of it.

"It's not far away, hopefully it will keep Father in the city and not out here." By the time he finished speaking the rain had come and it was coming down hard enough to make it impossible to speak as it splashed onto the rocks at the mouth of the cave.

We walked back into the cave and did what we do best; we found comfort in each other.

"Do you think it's safe in here?" I asked my mate, a gleam in my eye.

"Well, it's not like I'll turn into a vampire if a bat takes a nibble out of my ass." We both laughed at that, and he held me in his arms.

It had been a mad dash to get out of the city, and now this storm was holding us hostage in the cave. The air became warm the longer we stayed in there, and even the rock walls warmed up. I was leaning back against the wall, listening to the rain while I stroked my belly, when Malcolm pulled me close to his side.

"Whatever happens, Arista, I love you. You know that, right?" I couldn't see his face, but I knew from his voice that he was in serious-mode.

"I know, Malcolm. Maybe as much as I love you, you know?" It was the way I always teased him, but it deflected discussion of me, so I kept it up.

"I'm serious, my love. You are all I want in this world. You and our son." His hand went over my belly and I looked up to see his eyes in the near darkness.

"We'll be alright, darling. Don't worry."

"I just...damn my father." His head went back to the wall, and I could tell how frustrated he was by the tenseness in his jaw. "Why can't the man just leave us alone?"

"Would you, if it was our son? Would you let him carry on with a life you thought would destroy him?"

"I hadn't thought about it like that," he said, his eyes closing. "I don't know that I'd go to these lengths, but I do know I'll protect him no matter what it takes."

"And maybe your father feels the same way? Perhaps he thinks keeping us apart is for the best."

"Oh, he thinks you'll go berserk and kill all of us dragons, that's what you were made to do. You aren't a killer though, not even a dragon killer."

"Oh, don't be so quick to judge, dragon! I'll kill

anybody that threatens you or our child." I pulled away to make sure he saw how serious I was. I wasn't playing.

"I know, but that's different. Father thinks you'll go on a rampage. That's just crazy. You don't see the world that way."

"I don't, no, but I do think he's just trying to look out for you." It was a thought that had been bugging me since we got to this strange land.

I should hate Malcolm's father, I should definitely fear him, but once I'd learned about our baby, once I knew he really was growing away in my tummy, I'd started to understand him.

Godwin wasn't malicious, though I did think he'd gone a bit overboard. He was just a protective parent trying to keep his son from the dragon killer he thought I was. Alright, so his son loved me, Malcolm would get over that, right? He'd move on and have a family with another, far more suitable dragon female without these stabby-murdery tendencies, right?

Obviously, he didn't realize who his son was.

"Just, try to understand him a little, Malcolm. He's doing what he thinks is best." I couldn't believe I was defending the man.

Malcolm breathed out a long breath, before he stroked a hand over my shoulder again. "I guess you're right."

"I know I'm right. Now," I said, pushing up to look

him in the face, a smile on my own, "are we going to make use of this noisy storm or are we just going to sit here and worry about what we're going to do next?"

"By rights, we should be panicking right now, Arista. We have no money, no food, and no way out of this place."

"Don't forget our new home is a cave, babe." I waved a hand around and grinned. "Great, isn't it?"

"I don't know how you can be so cheerful." He groused for a moment longer, but I shut him up with a kiss.

I needed the distraction as much as he did, and the one place I found completely distracting was a place only Malcolm could take me to. We didn't bother to take our clothes off, the floor was too gritty with sand and we'd both been sweating buckets, but that didn't matter. Buttons opened, mouths fused, and fingers stroked until we were both panting heavily in the secluded little cave.

He was right, we should have been worrying, we should have been planning, but if I did any of that I'd feel overwhelmed, so I chose to ride him into a mind-scorching orgasm. I'd panic later.

Malcolm, always so careful with me, pulled me on top of his body, and I sank down onto him, my pink dress fluttering around us to hide what we were doing. My fingers gripped at his bare chest, his shirt up around his neck now that I'd pushed it up, and I lost myself in how good it felt to have him fill me.

Malcolm joined me in that place, and for a moment, his father, the world, and everything else stopped existing. There was only us, intertwined once again in total completion.

It didn't take long before we noticed the rain had stopped and Malcolm went out to look for wood that might have escaped the downpour. No doubt it would get cold in the cave after the sun went down, even if we were in a hot climate. Besides, the light would keep away wild animals.

I heard noises outside of the cave about twenty minutes after he'd gone and went out to see if he needed help carrying the wood in. The sight that greeted me wasn't Malcolm, though, it was a tribe of women. They were dressed in the same style of linen shifts, an A-line shape that covered their bodies but wouldn't be hot.

They all looked similar in that they had tanned skin, black hair, and brown eyes, but their facial features were all different. Two had flat, wide noses, another had a slim nose and full lips, while the fourth had thin lips, a short nose, wider cheekbones than the others, or a round face where the others had oval faces. They might be cousins, but they weren't all the same.

"Hello, can I help you?" I didn't assume they spoke English, I just hoped they did.

"Join us, sister, while the dragon is gone. Hurry, before he comes back!" The woman in the lead, the one with the round face and lighter eyes than the others, came to me and tried to beckon me away from the cave.

"What? He's my mate, there's no need to worry about him." I waved off her worry and made to sit on a rock. "Would you like…"

I paused, because I had nothing to offer.

"No, sister, you can't be mate to the dragon. You are a hunter. Come now, please. We can take you to safety."

I stared at her because I'd noticed that the movement of her lips and what I was hearing were far different, like a movie that was out of sync. Was she speaking a different language and my brain was interpreting it as English?

"I'm fine, seriously. But I could use some food if you have it." I patted my belly, my little boy inside kicking away in protest at the lack of nourishment.

"He has put a spell on her. Salvia, Juniper, take her. We must go before the dragon comes back."

"What?" I'd been paying more attention to her mouth, fascinated with the fact that I knew she wasn't saying those words, than to what she was saying.

I stood up, my arms raised defensively as the two women came towards me. When one of the women in the back brought out a spear tip and held it to my neck, I stopped fighting. No use dying if it wouldn't protect my baby, right?

"Hurry, Juniper," the leader said to the woman tying a rope around my wrists.

They pulled me through the jungle, deep into the heart of it, and my spirits were flagging. I'd had a mad dash through the city, a bit of adult fun with Malcolm, and I was tired. Another trek was the last thing I wanted. I wanted a nap, some food, and something cold to drink.

"This is the city of the dragon hunters, sister. You will be safe here."

I stared out at a city that reminded me of ruins I'd seen in pictures from Mexico. The jungle had been cleared out to make room for the humans, and now there were women and female children wandering the streets, talking as if I hadn't just been kidnapped and the day was normal.

I walked into the city with round eyes and a thumping heart. What had I gotten into now?

17

MALCOLM

I made my way back to the cave, calling out for Arista to let her know I was back. When she didn't come out, I thought she must be asleep and went inside. The sun was going down now and the cave was only growing darker.

I placed my feet carefully as I went. I didn't want to kick her in the dark, so I moved with caution. I'd covered the entire cave without finding her. Where was she?

I went back out to the front of the cave but didn't see her. I glared into the darkness, and moved around, thinking perhaps she'd gone to use the "outside facilities", but she wasn't there. She simply was not there! Where was she?

I looked around and felt like the world was starting to spin when she didn't appear. I fell to the ground, panic making me hyperventilate. Arista was gone and I had no idea where she was. Had she run off? Had my father taken her?

Surely he would have stayed behind for me if he'd been the one to take her? I ran back to the cave entrance, looking around for any clues. I found a soft leather scrap of cloth that had been kicked to one side that hadn't been there before. Near the outcrop of rocks, the cloth had a symbol on it that made my blood run cold.

Dragon hunters.

There were dragon hunters here, this scrap proved it. Two dragons locked in combat but caged within a circle, the symbol of the hunters of old. They knew I was here, and they'd obviously taken the one they'd considered their own. Would they harm her? How had I not sensed them?

Maybe it was that potion, I thought, as I sat down once more. Looking into the coming darkness, I knew something had blocked me sensing them here. We'd thought they were all gone, but it would seem they'd just gone into hiding, right under the noses of those they hunted. Were these untrained as Arista had been?

She'd gone with them, so obviously they'd either taken her or convinced her to go. I knew she wouldn't go without me, so I doubted she'd just traipsed off happily with them. No, they must be aware of what they were, of what I was, and had come to save Arista. Why not attack me, I wondered? Maybe they weren't strong enough.

I knew there was little chance of finding Arista, but I went out into the jungle anyway. I followed the path we'd thought was just an animal trail, but now I had to wonder because it seemed to be a special place. If the dragon hunters had found Arista so easily, perhaps the cave was a sacred place to them.

I looked throughout the night, wishing my powers would come back so I could take flight and look for her from the air. Henry had said that the potion was wearing off and I kept trying but I couldn't shift. I felt helpless, the same as I'd felt in the prison because I couldn't help Arista, I didn't even know for sure where she was. Depression became a heavy weight on my mind. I felt like I'd failed her again.

I avoided the sounds of animals and the slithering of snakes in the trees as I walked through the dense forest. This was not a safe place, not like I'd thought it was when we had first walked into it fleeing from my father. In the darkness, it seemed even more sinister than the plans my father had for us. I did not know what kind of animals lay in the dark, or what might be in the trees waiting to devour me, but I was not totally helpless.

Even without my powers, I was still strong and I still had the skills that I'd been trained with. I simply couldn't shift into a dragon or use the senses that I had when I was in my dragon. I had almost become human and it didn't feel that bad. I was worried the dragon hunters would be able to overpower me, but I didn't care. All that mattered was getting to Arista and getting her to safety.

The sun was starting to rise by the time I smelled the first hint of smoke. There was a village close by, and I hoped it was the right village. I was exhausted from my trek through the jungle, covered in mosquito bites, hungry, and dehydrated but that didn't stop me. Even without my dragon powers I knew that Arista was close, I could feel her.

Those first niggling pains of separation had started during the night. That tight ache had started in my chest and squeezed my stomach, and it was already making me tense by the time I smelled the smoke. I moved carefully to the few trees at the border of what I thought was a village. I came to a wide tree and stared out into the distance.

There was no way I'd be able to get Arista out of the city which stood before me. Torches lit the buildings up. Every building and every floor had a torch. It almost looked like a modern city at first, because there were so many lights. The rising sun showed me it was full of people.

It looked like an Aztec city or a Mayan ruin, but it

was in the middle of the jungle of a magical world and was, perhaps, even bigger than the place we'd run from. I didn't know where to start, so I watched for a while. I didn't see any men, only women and children as the women began their morning routines. The women were taking down the torches and putting them out while the children were passing out baskets of bread. They left the baskets at doorsteps and knocked before they moved on to the next door.

I watched as each door was opened by a woman; I didn't see any men at all. This was some kind of matriarchal society and yet that didn't mean that I could just go in and take Arista. These were women who knew how to protect themselves and they'd been here for generations from the looks of the place.

I started through alleyways, keeping an eye out for anyone who might spot me. I made my way to the center of the city just in time to see the slanting of sun rays as the sun brightened the sky. Women were gathered there already doing their work for the day. From what I could see it looked like they were training for battle, but none held weapons or wore protective clothing.

The sun blinded me for a moment as it continued to climb in the sky, but I was certain I had seen Arista. They were bringing her from one of the thatched roof houses that dotted the area around the main pyramid in the middle. Everything flowed from the pyramid: avenues, the round houses with thatched roofs, water wells, and stalls for selling goods—it all flowed outwards from the pyramid.

I looked to see where Arista was once more and saw that they were leading her to the pyramid. I didn't know anything about this culture, and it seemed unlikely they were taking her as a sacrifice but it wasn't beyond the realm of possibility. I felt my power surge suddenly through my veins and wanted to shift immediately but I still couldn't.

Suddenly voices broke the quiet of the waking city, a shout that I knew translated to dragon. Women of all ages surged around me, but I still couldn't shift. It reminded me of the one time I'd tried to drive a car but the engine wouldn't turn over. It would work if I could just get that one little bit of power through, but it just wouldn't come through. I tried to remain calm as I looked at the sea of unfamiliar female faces.

"You are too late, dragon, we are sending her home. That's where she belongs, not with you. How dare you defile a hunter like that? She does not even realize what she is, not truly." A woman broke through the sea of faces and came towards me. Her face was creased with disgust and again I wondered at a world where two people who loved each other could not be together based on old prejudices.

"She is my mate, hunter. We cannot undo what fate has deemed to be perfection." I stared her down, watching as the women began to take battle stances. Some were crouched in front of me as if they would pounce on me, while others near the back began to pick up rocks. I might not get out of this alive.

"That is impossible, dragon. Why would fate decide that a dragon and a dragon hunter should be mates? That makes no sense."

I looked up at the pyramid as a sound like thunder cracked through the air. A portal had opened at the top of the pyramid, a circular shape of distorted air appeared there. I saw Arista being pushed through the portal, and even from this distance, I could hear her shout my name.

"No, you can't send her back! My father will kill her or take her prisoner. On top of that, we will die without each other."

"You are not mated," the dragon hunter sneered. "It is impossible. You will not die without her and she will not die without you. What will happen is she will go on to live a normal life, as a normal human. Without you or your filth defiling her."

For the second time in my life, I heard these terms used to describe Arista and me. I wanted to scream at the injustice of it, but I knew there was little I could do. My fate was uncertain but I was certain of one thing: if I couldn't shift I was about to die, and that meant Arista would die as well.

The leader menaced towards me, watching me intently. I knew Arista was gone and I knew where she would be, as for the 500th time that day I tried to shift. Power surged through me, wiping away my exhaustion, as finally something went right for me. I kicked off from the ground. The screams of anger from below mattered little to me. If I hadn't been in my dragon shape I would have shouted with glee.

Instead, I flew as fast as I could, as high as I could to get away from the death that awaited me below. I soared into the rising sun, aiming for the clouds, and flexed the muscles that hadn't been used for months. It was not normal for a dragon to go so long without shifting, but it didn't show as my tail sailed out behind me, my rudder to guide my way through the wind.

I headed for the familiar, away from the land of the eternal sun and sand. I didn't head home or towards Arista's home. I flew to a place where I knew I could seek refuge, the land where pineapples and lava ruled. Over the ocean I flew, a streak of black and red that human eyes would not see. I had no plans other than to get there, regroup, and figure out a way to get to Arista. My father would have people there, I just knew it, and I would not be able to help her if we were both imprisoned.

My instinct, of course, was to fly straight to her, but I knew better. Love can make you do stupid things, but sometimes it was better to wait and go in with a plan. I was sensible enough to know that.

I was near to the chain of islands when I began to descend to the ground. I didn't get far before my flight down was halted. My father and my own security team —a team I'd trained myself—interrupted my descent and captured me with a net of silver alloy. I wouldn't be scarred by the alloy, but I was contained as the net was painful against my skin. The burns would heal much better than if the net had been made of pure silver. I plummeted to the ground, a tight ball, and lay there defeated at last. I couldn't even try to fight anymore. Exhaustion took me the moment I'd shifted back into human form when I hit the ground.

The effort to shift had drained me completely after my night of trekking through the jungle. A priest came and created a portal for us to travel through, and I was dragged away in my silver chains, but no one said a word. There were no congratulations, no laughs of triumph. It was just a security team quietly taking in a prisoner.

I went peacefully to the prison cell where my father had kept me previously. The fight had left me for now.

"He can live without his hunter now," I heard my

father saying to someone. I was too exhausted to lift my head to answer or to question him in any way.

The last of the world left me when a needle pricked my arm and the flames of a million fires began to burn in my blood. I didn't know it, but I screamed the scream of the damned, a scream that made everyone in the room cringe with sympathy. Everyone but my father.

"This should take care of that little problem of his. You can destroy the hunter now. And that abomination she carries." The satisfaction in his voice should have had me up off the bed with my hands around his throat, but I was too busy being consumed with the agony of having my mating torn away from me. Curled up into a ball on the bed, all I could think was that I would die from the agony of it, and perhaps that was a blessing.

18

ARISTA

stepped through the portal that Juniper directed me to, my blood pounding in my ears with fear. She'd explained it was a portal that would take me home, but what would it do to me? More importantly, what would it do to my child?

She insisted it was safe, so I took a step towards it. She was behind me, almost pushing me because I was so hesitant to go through. I heard a shout as I took another step, heard the cry of "dragon!". I looked around frantically until I saw Malcolm standing at the bottom of the pyramid surrounded by women. Women who had been trained to kill him.

I tried to move, to step away, but Juniper pushed me through the portal and I was tripping into my own world before I knew it. I caught myself on a tree and looked around. Whoever made those portals was good at what they did. I was in the forest not far from my mother's house. I began to walk towards my mother's home, but my steps slowed as I came near it.

The sun was just coming up here, it was breaking over the horizon, and the foggy mist that can often be found in the mountains on cold mornings was coming up from the valley below. It didn't look any different here, and it was still cold. I had been gone for months and it was still cold. It should have been warm by now. What was going on?

By now my stomach was big enough that I was beginning to waddle a little when I walked, and I put my hands to my back to try to ease the ache there. Mom sure did have a surprise in store for her when she saw me. I picked up the pace as I neared the house and I found the key that she always hid in a potted plant.

I was in the kitchen pouring a glass of orange juice when my mother came in, a double barrel shotgun in her hands pointing straight at me.

"Mom," I shrieked, fear sending a lance of pain through my belly. "What are you doing?"

"Arista?" My mother's eyes immediately welled with tears as she stared at me in shock. "Baby, you're home?"

I ran to her, taking her in my arms after she put the shotgun down safely, and kissed her cheeks.

"I'm home, Mom."

She pulled away, her eyes racing over my face while her hands checked my limbs for injury.

"Where have you been? And what is this?" Her hands were over my stomach cradling the child within.

"That's my baby, Mom. You'll get to meet him in around four more months." I gave her a grin of pure happiness. I should have been sad and maybe even weeping, but I hadn't seen my mom in so long and we were together again. I should probably have been terrified, I'd left Malcolm when he was surrounded by a city full of hunters, but I had faith in him. I also thought I'd be feeling pain or sickness if he was dead. I wouldn't worry until I felt something and right now I didn't, so I was determined to enjoy being reunited with my mother.

"Where have you been, honey?" She led me to the table and we sat down together.

As the sun filled the room with light, I began to see the toll my disappearance had taken on her. The skin beneath her eyes was bruised, and her cheeks had sunken in. She'd lost a lot of weight too, and I felt guilty for causing her worry.

"I don't know how to explain it, Mom," How could I? "I've just been gone and right now I can't tell you a whole lot about where I've been."

"Honey, you don't know what's happened. Your father, well, your father has had me charged with your kidnapping and murder. He thinks I went crazy and killed you the night you disappeared. Willow tried to explain that she would have heard if I'd done anything to you because she was there with you, but nobody would listen. I've just..." Her words trailed off as she began to wring her hands. "They all think I'm crazy. Everybody in this town, and all those lawyers, them people from the city, them reporters." She paused through a sob before she pushed it down and started to speak again. "All of them think I'm crazy and that I killed you. My trial starts next week. Luckily, Anna was able to get me out of jail and hire me a lawyer."

"What? What the hell, Mom? Oh my God! What the fuck is wrong with Dad?" I stared at her in horror before I stood up and began to pace around the kitchen, not noticing the amount of swearing I was doing. Mom didn't reprimand me, so I kept on.

"Oh God, when I find him, I'm going to wring his fucking neck. How dare he?"

"Honey, he was only afraid." She paused to search for the right words. "If I hadn't seen you go off with that dragon, I'd have been worried too. I guess that's part of it, why they think I'm crazy. I told them all you'd gone off with the dragon and none of them believed me. I guess it's to be expected nowadays, people don't believe in dragons anymore."

"Mom, we have to fix this. Dad might have done this

out of the good of his heart but putting you in prison for murder is just crazy. Crazier than they think you are. Apparently, that's a whole lot of crazy."

"Now baby, don't be mad at your dad. He's been grief-stricken since you disappeared. He's had a hard life you know, first a crazy wife, and then his daughter disappears. It's not been easy on him. He's only done the best he knew how to do, and he's done that out of love."

I sat back down, finishing off my orange juice. "I guess so but I'm still mad at him. Imagine thinking that you killed me. What a load of horse sh—"

But I stopped myself that time.

I spent the rest of the day at the police station making sure they knew I was alive. I kept my story simple and told them I needed a break. I've been ill, I informed them, and I just needed some time to myself. The police chief kept looking at my belly, and I knew he had questions, but he kept them to himself.

It seems I was only gone from my world for three months, definitely not long enough to have a belly of this size, but I guess they knew there was a man involved if I was pregnant. I kept the truth to myself and didn't volunteer any information that wasn't necessary. By late that afternoon, I was back at Mom's and she was making us dinner. All of the charges against her had been dropped of course. I had yet to see my father.

The days began to pass as they always did, and the

sickness of being separated from Malcolm started to take a toll. The child within me helped to ease some of it, so the signs were slower this time, but it was still happening. I'd been worried that Malcolm's father would come for me, but I hadn't let that stop me making sure that Mom stayed out of jail.

Weeks began to pass instead of just days, and Mom tried to find a way to get me back to Malcolm. She was the only one who knew the real story, but this she kept to herself for a change. She and Dad had been seeing more of each other, and I was hopeful for a reconciliation.

I heard them talking out on the porch one night. The nights getting warmer now, and I heard him admit for the first time that maybe he'd been wrong. He still thought her dragon talk was crazy, but he didn't think she was dangerous or ever had been. It was a start, at least.

My pregnancy slowed down to match the time of the world I was in, and between that and the mating sickness, I was having a hard time staying awake. I spent a lot of time dreaming about Malcolm, wondering where he was, but we had no idea how to get me there to him.

Willow, miraculously, was still clinging to life. She could still walk, and her mother would bring her to sit with me often. One night, when I was particularly tired, she decided to stay the night so that we could binge watch terrible movies from the 1980s. We were watching a rather raunchy movie about boys trying to get into a strip club when we heard a tap at my window.

I ran to the window, hoping it was Malcolm, but it was only Henry. Henry only had eyes for Willow, which I found intriguing, but I was more concerned with where Malcolm was.

"What are you doing here, Henry?" I asked, looking behind him to see if Malcolm was there.

"He's not here but he will be soon. Take this," he said quickly, handing over some kind of amulet on a necklace. "Keep this on you at all times. It will keep you and the child safe."

He could not take his eyes from my cousin and I couldn't help but smile when I looked back to see her just as engrossed. Perhaps Henry was her mate? I could see color coming back into her face and her skin beginning to soften. The lines were disappearing as the minutes passed. I'd found her mate at last. I wanted to dance with the excitement of it all, Malcolm was coming, and my cousin had found her mate!

"Henry, do you want—" I began, but he cut me off.

"No, no. I don't have time, Arista, I have to go. But Malcolm will be here soon, so be ready for him." He started to turn away before he turned back. "Who is she?"

I smiled because he could still not take his eyes from her.

"She is my beautiful cousin, Willow. And if you would like to come in I could properly introduce you." I blinked my eyelashes at him comically, a smile wide enough to make my face ache.

"I'd love to, but I really must go." His captivated expression told me that was a lie. I had to suppress the urge to dance again. I knew how they both felt, what they were thinking, and most of all, I knew if I could get him back here, Willow would improve tremendously!

Henry gulped loudly and caught my attention once again. "Father does not know my part in this and I would rather he did not learn about it. just keep the amulet safe until Malcolm gets here and give it to him. He'll know what to do with it. Maybe... maybe I can come back and tell your cousin how everything progresses. Later of course, not right now, because I have to go. But she is so beautiful... I have to go. Good night to both of you."

With that, he was gone into the night. I swear he was blushing when he shifted, and I had to laugh at just how distracted he'd been by my cousin. I was elated because I knew that Malcolm was coming for me at last. I'd waited so long and now it was almost over.

I went back to the bed and now my cousin really wanted to know the truth. I began the long tale, telling her how I'd met Malcolm, about the mating sickness, and how he'd cured me. I didn't tell her I thought Henry was her mate, just in case, but I saw her glancing at the window. I think she already knew the answer to that. The sky was starting to get light by the time I finished.

We pulled the covers up to our chins and Willow was already asleep by the time I was over my excitement enough to close my eyes. It had been a long time coming, and I didn't know what the end result was going to be of our latest effort to be together, but I was happy because Malcolm was coming.

I don't know how much longer Godwin would try to stalk us, I just hoped he'd leave us in peace soon enough. With the baby coming, and the last few months of continually being on edge, I was really starting to feel burdened. I loved Malcolm, he was my true mate and my love. I loved that I carried his child and that we were going to be a family. But I could do without the interference from his father.

That part was getting old quickly. I turned to Willow and threw an arm over her skinny waist. Henry was going to have his work cut out getting her back to health, but if he was anything like his brother, I knew he could do it. If his father let him, that was. Having two dragon hunters in the family might just make the man's head explode. It served him right, I thought, as sleep started to make my brain foggy. Acting like I was scum just because I was a hunter. I was carrying his grand-child for goodness sake.

I suspected that was one of the reasons he'd left me alone so far. I didn't think the child was completely human, not if Malcolm could talk to him. Maybe he was only half-shifter? That would be terrible if only half of him shifted! Malcolm had explained to me that if he was half-shifter, our baby might not be able to shift but he'd have other powers. I hoped so. In a world of ghosts, vampires, and shifters, I thought my child was going to be a target. That meant I needed his father. Hopefully, Henry was right, and I'd have Malcolm back soon.

I fell into sleep at last, too exhausted to think anymore.

MALCOLM

I spent two days in a stupor of agony. The injection burned like acid as it coursed through my veins. My father left me to scream the pain away. He did not come near me in that time. He left me, breaking and broken.

Arista was gone, and I knew she must be safe because I didn't feel a parting from her. I could still feel her as part of my soul, so I knew the injection hadn't worked. Father may have dreamed of freeing me from my mating but it was still only a dream.

When the screaming stopped, I was brought food and fresh clothing, but I was still a prisoner. I was his prisoner again. I didn't want his kingdom at all now, I just wanted my mate and our child, and to be left in peace. I didn't really want to be king, as I'd told Arista. If being king drives you to torture your child, it was a hell

I didn't want to know.

It was weeks before my father came to see me at last, and he made the mistake of coming into my cell. I launched myself at him with an angry scream of rage. My hands went directly around his throat, squeezing and crushing the life from him. He'd tried to steal my life, Arista's life, and the life of my child; he was no longer my father. He was my Tormentor.

My father was not an old man for his age, he was still young for a dragon. He was king because he was the strongest of us all. It didn't take much for him to fend me off, despite my size and my training. I'd seen a flash of fear in his eyes though, and I think the fact that I attacked him—that his *child* attacked him—finally broke through his prejudice.

"It didn't work then?" He sank down against the wall of my prison, and I knew he felt defeated.

"Not that I know of. You did keep forgetting the one truth in all of this. The one thing I kept trying to tell you. I love her and that goes well beyond even the mating bond. Even if you broke our bond, you couldn't destroy the fact we love each other."

"I suppose I couldn't," he said with his head against the wall, his eyes closed. "I tried but it wasn't out of spite. I only wanted to protect you."

"There comes a time when you have to let go of your children, that time should have been before you had us put in prison, but now would work as well. You're never going to win, Father, you can't destroy what we have."

"Then go, son." His voice was tired, as broken as I'd felt in the past. "I only wanted what was best for you."

"That wasn't good enough, Father. That's not good enough now. It isn't enough to explain what you've done to us. You have to look inside yourself to find the right answer. It's not just their world that is changing, our world is changing too. The child Arista carries will be a blending of those two worlds and we can hope that we can merge the two at last."

"Ah, but you're forgetting the wolves, my son. They are knocking at our door and insisting we let them in. They think the times are changing too, and they want to change everything about our world, including the rulers."

"That will have to be a fight for another day. Today I'm going to my mate I'm going to make sure she's safe. I will come back to help fight the wolves if you need me. I will not be king here, though. Henry is probably better suited to that than me. Goodbye, Father."

Then I left him and walked out of my cell.

I thought about his words as I flew over the ocean to Arista. I didn't know exactly what was going on with the wolves, I'd been out of the loop for far too long, but it didn't sound good. There may be a battle coming, but it was one they wouldn't win if I had anything to do with it.

I felt Arista before I saw her, her tie with our child only made our bond stronger. She was standing outside of her mother's home when I landed. Unlike the other times, this time both of her parents were waiting with her. Her father was almost comical in his astonishment as I landed. I held back laughter until she was in my arms and I forgot that I wanted to laugh.

"Oh… ohhhhh. That's a…" I could almost swear his eyes were going to roll back in his head and he was going to faint, but Ted held it together.

"Good man," I said with a proud grin. I extended my hand to him and he just stared at me, so I dropped it. "I'm Malcolm, Arista's mate."

"Hi. I'm Eve, her mother, and this is Ted." I knew their names, Arista had told me already, but it was nice to have this formal introduction.

"It's a pleasure to meet you," I purred to her and she giggled. Ted was still staring, unable to believe his eyes.

"Well, shall we go inside?" Arista asked, her eyes only on me.

"Yes, I insist on getting a few facts from you, young man," Eve said to me, her eyes narrowing. "You won't be running off with my daughter again, without telling me a little bit about where you're going and how long you plan to be gone."

"Mom—" Arista began.

"No, it's fine Arista," I said. "We have all the time in the world." That's when it finally sank in that we were really free. My father would not try to stop us now and we really could have a life. "We can stay here in your world, or we can explore the many different worlds of mine and take our time. There's no rush anymore."

"If we can stay here for a little bit I know Mom and Dad both have questions. And I think it's time I had some answers."

That's how I found myself sitting at a kitchen table, coffee cup in hand, as I explained the dragon world and what exactly Eve and Arista were. I did not sugarcoat my race's past or try to pretend we were right when we'd stolen women, but that wasn't who the dragon community was now. We didn't steal women or children anymore.

Although if the rumors I'd heard before my incarceration were true, the wolves might be. That was something else that would have to be dealt with. For now, I could barely keep my eyes off Arista.

She was a beautiful woman, there was no doubt of that, and she held my attention. Her beauty went deeper than the surface; it went straight to her bones. Her beauty came from her love of her family, and her love of me. Now that love included our child. It went further than that too, though. She was just a kind, good person that wanted to only experience what life had to offer. She was going to get that chance now.

Ted had been quiet throughout the night, but he seemed to wake up suddenly, because he shook himself and looked over at Eve.

"I've been terrible to you."

"I can't blame you, Ted. The rest of the world stood in line with you. I'm crazy."

"But you aren't, that's just it. You never were. You were actually the sane one!" He was astounded all over again, and I couldn't blame him.

"To be fair to you, Ted, we did withdraw from your world and left them here."

"Didn't you say there was some in that other world, Ris? Some of us?" Eve broke in, her eyes on Arista.

"Yes, but they'd hidden away in plain sight, so to speak. They were happy to live in peace, I think." She looked thoughtful, and I knew we'd be visiting that place someday. We had a lot to do to change people's minds about the dragon-hunter dichotomy, but we would do it.

At least, in my world. I still didn't think the human world was ready to find out that dragons, shifters, and ghosts are real.

"I'll get that," Ted said when a knock interrupted our conversation.

I was surprised to see Henry at the door. I stood up and looked at him in question.

"I've just come to, uh, check that you're alright. Father said he's not going to pursue you anymore." His cheeks turned red.

"That's good news. Why are you blushing? Stop being silly and have a seat." I pointed at the chair Arista had pulled out for him. I liked this sitting at a kitchen table and discussing things activity. We didn't do that in my world. Kitchens were far away, full of screaming, sweaty people, and not my cup of tea in general.

Henry turned even redder and sat down, his eyes searching the room and landing on Arista. "And your cousin, Willow, how is she?"

Ah, a woman, that explained it!

"She's at home, Henry. I don't know how she is, but she was the same as she was last night when I saw her."

Arista gave him a smile I recognized. She knew something he didn't want to admit. Had we found her cousin's mate? My father would have a heart attack!

"Is that all Henry?" I changed the subject, letting my younger brother find a way out of his quandary.

"I'm to tell you that you may still be king, as you may change your mind in the time before Father passes into eternity. You will always be welcome in our home no matter what you decide."

"That's a complete about-face then. Wow!" Arista spoke up, her voice sharp.

We were both angry at Father, but she'd been right in that he'd been trying to protect me. It would take time, maybe a lot of time, but I think we would both let that anger go in the future. Maybe.

"And the amulet?" Arista asked, holding out a gold amulet on a necklace.

"That's for both of you. It will keep evil from you. Bad intentions, stuff like that. So Alec says, anyway," Henry rushed to tell us.

I took the amulet and saw that it was covered with runes. A triangle shaped thing, it wasn't pretty, but it was full of power. I gave it back to my mate and she put it in her pocket. She needed the protection more than I did. It would be one more thing to keep her and our son safe.

"Right then, if that's all the questions and the schedule is set…" I pointed at the piece of paper on the table, something Arista's mother insisted on. She wanted to be present for the birth and visits in between and after. She wasn't going to let her daughter out of her sight again.

We'd had to perform some rather complicated math, but I think we had the dates right now.

"You're leaving already? But you only just got here." Ted stood up, his hands out for Arista's.

"We'll be back soon, Dad. I promise. We just need some time together. We haven't been able to really have a chance to be together without some worry in the back of our heads, or a time where we've not been running. It won't be long. I promise."

We might be, I thought to myself with a growl as she stood up and hugged her parents and said goodbye. We were finally free, and I was going to spend every moment making love to her that she'd let me.

We left them with smiles and a wave before I shifted and carried her off to the paradise I'd been heading for when my father captured me. I landed in a world of greens and yellows. The light even had a green tint to it here.

I found a place on the beach where soft, thick green leaves formed a bed and the canopy of the trees protected us. The ocean rushed in and receded from the beach, adding a soft, soothing sound to our retreat.

"I love you so much, Arista," I said as I shifted and went to her. My fingers traced from her cheek to her chin, and she looked at me hungrily.

"I love you more, dragon," she whispered, just before she pressed her lips into me.

This time we weren't slow, we didn't have the patience for driving each other up so high we'd scream until we fell down the other side. Oh no, there was no time for that at all.

I backed my mate up to a tree and stripped her clothes from her, one at a time, until they were gone. She took mine off too, and before long we were both naked and her legs were around my hips.

I was buried in her wet heat, searching for oblivion, but I wanted her to join me there. She'd been ready for me when I hiked her up the tree and thrust into her. Hot, wet, and silky smooth, her walls had sucked me into her greedily. Now, I wanted to lose myself in her oblivion, but not without her.

I pulled myself together, planted my feet more firmly in the sand and slid a hand between us. I flicked at her clit until she moaned my name, her head lazily resting on my shoulder as I fucked into her.

"Wake up, princess. Watch me fuck you." I breathed it against her neck, and she was soon staring straight into my eyes. "Watch as I fuck the world away for us both."

Her pupils dilated and her eyes went round, but she looked at me. She couldn't see past her stomach, but I held her steady with one hand as she looked into my eyes.

"I want to fuck you for the rest of my life," she whispered, her eyes going tight for a minute as she grew closer.

She made a purring sound as I sank once more, hard and deep, into her slick walls. I wanted to come immediately but held it back. When she started to pant my name and her walls clenched around me, I knew I was gone. I tried to hold back but Arista's sweet little pussy sucked me into letting go.

We'd have time for slow, gentle lovemaking later. Right now, I just wanted to come inside of her as she exploded around me with quick little gasps of my name.

Over and over, she said my name, her fingers clenching dangerously hard into my back as she bit into my shoulder. My mate came apart around me, and the world was right at last.

20

ARISTA

*L*ife on the island was perfect. It took me a while to get used to the light being green but other than that, it was a beautiful place. It was like Hawaii only it was as if someone had jazzed it up. The trees moved when you moved so you'd always be in shade. The birds sang beautifully from each branch. Every aspect was perfect.

The birdsong was my favorite part of the place. It moved me, it touched my soul with pure sounds that resonated within me, and it made me glad to be alive. Sometimes it made me cry, and I began to realize that the birdsong wasn't for me. The birds were singing their emotions. As my pregnancy progressed, even the sweet songs could make me cry.

I was close to my time, I suspected that by my size, but I wasn't completely sure. It was hard to tell when time passed differently in all of the worlds. I started to think of them as tears in the space-time continuum. Some places time passed quickly, in others it crawled by. You weren't aware of it when you were in the world because time seemed to move at a normal pace, but it wasn't in sync with everywhere else.

We went back many times to my world, to visit my parents and to see my family. My cousin never talked about Henry when I was with her, but I knew something was happening because she was getting better. Willow did not improve as quickly as I did, so I suspected they were not actually seeing each other, but something was happening. She was even able to get back to playing the piano a couple of weeks after Henry first saw her.

She had color back in her skin, and she didn't look as old as she used to. She looked normal and beautiful all over again. Even her hair came back to life and fell in silky waves down her back. I hadn't told her I thought Henry was her mate, but I think she suspected.

I'm part of the magical world now, even though I have no magical skills of my own. The birds have magic, and the trees have magic, a magic that Malcolm can share with them. He makes fire with his hands and talks to the trees and birds to bring us food. It really is a magical world.

I'd stopped wearing clothes because we were the only ones doing so on the island, and I had nothing to be ashamed of. Malcolm sometimes wore a loincloth made of leaves to protect his delicate parts from the sun, but I didn't bother. I enjoyed being naked in my pregnancy. When we went back to my world and I had to wear clothes I felt like I was smothered, and I was tense until we returned to our island where I could take them off again.

The island was an old place in an older world and we explored every inch. We didn't know how long it had been uninhabited, so we explored it like two children hoping to find pirate treasure. We didn't need money, but if we needed it we could always get it from Malcolm's father. He hadn't seen his father since he was released, and I couldn't blame him. I understood his father's reasoning but that didn't mean I accepted it. Especially since we were the ones he'd imprisoned.

I was walking through the forest, my hands trailing along glossy leaves of banana trees, when I felt the first pain. It felt like cramps, something I hadn't felt in a while but was all too familiar with. I'd heard your first labor could take hours or even days so I didn't rush back to the area we'd set up as our home. I breathed through the pain until it disappeared and kept walking. I didn't go so far that I couldn't hear the waves crashing on the beach anymore, but I was a good distance from the tree-house Malcolm had built for us.

Another pain had me on my knees within minutes,

and I screamed for Malcolm. He came tearing through the jungle to find my back arched as I screamed out in my pain. I felt like my bones were breaking apart in my pelvis, as though my muscles were tearing strand by strand.

"Fuck me, this hurts!" I groaned as a wave of pain passed.

"What did you do?" he almost wailed, and I laughed.

"Well, a few months ago, I met this dragon and he was super-hot so I fu—"

"The baby's coming?" He looked excited but terrified at the same time.

"Yes," I panted as another wave started. "Fuck, Malcolm!"

I screeched through that one too, but he still picked me up and flew us back to camp in his dragon form.

"No, no, no, take me to my mother, Malcolm, we promised!" I managed through waves of pain.

"What if he shoots out of you while we're over the water and he drowns? I'll go and get her." He started to turn, but I stopped him.

"Have you never seen a birth?" I asked, looking at him with disbelief.

"No," he said, looking sheepish.

"Not even when you could watch it online?" I really couldn't believe this.

"No, I was afraid to watch it."

I'd have shouted at him if I wasn't on my knees screaming in pain in the next instant. "Take me to my mother!"

He flew us faster than he'd ever flown before and ran into Mom's house with me bouncing in his arms. She had my bedroom ready for the event and went into mid-wife mode. As a woman in the mountains, she'd helped women give birth when roads were too bad to get to hospitals or during other emergencies. She could handle this, as long as it wasn't too complicated.

I began to panic as the waves started to come faster. What if the baby was a monster? What if was human but had green skin? Malcolm knew my thoughts and tried to assure me our baby wasn't going to come out green, but this was a birth unlike any before, how did he know?

"You're right, I don't know, Arista, but we'll love this baby no matter what." He cringed a little as I thought about a little green, horned monster coming out of me.

It felt like the baby was covered in razors as it moved through my birth canal, and I screamed my pain and panic again.

"It's okay, my love, it's okay." He soothed me with a song and placed a cold wet washcloth on my forehead.

I gritted my teeth through the hours when Mom told me not to push and paced in between the contractions. They were coming constantly now, so I was standing in front of the bed, crouched down with my hands braced above my head on a bar Mom had installed.

"I don't know why they make women give birth lying down on their backs now, that's just silly. Stand up, Arista, come on baby, don't sink down like that, you'll squish the top of the baby's head when it comes out." Mom wasn't trying to be comical, just matter of fact, but she made me laugh anyway.

When the pains became too much for me to endure Malcolm wanted to get a magical midwife.

"By the time you get there and back Malcolm, I think this will be over with," my mother told him, eyeing my not-so-private parts clinically. "Go in the kitchen and pace with Ted. Go on now, you're getting on my nerves, boy."

My mother did have a way with words, I thought, as I laughed again. To me, she only whispered love and encouragement. She periodically checked to see if the baby was crowning, and I was happy it was my mother sharing such an intimate moment with me.

"I'm glad we decided against the hospital, Mom." I gritted my teeth. "Not just because if the baby is born a dragon they'll ask questions, but because I get to share this with you. We missed so much of each other's lives, I don't want you to miss anything of this baby's life."

"Oh, I'll miss parts just because we live so far away from each other, but that's the only reason. Now concentrate on birthing this baby, Arista, and let's meet your son."

I grinned a grin that was probably macabre because it was mixed with pain, and finally began the exhausting part of birthing my child. I pushed when Mom told me to and rested in between. My fists knotted on the bar over the bed and she rubbed my back. It took hours, days, weeks it felt like, but it was only minutes before I heard my child screaming his entry into the world.

Malcolm came running into the room just as our boy slipped from my body, and he caught him. Mom did the necessary cleaning up and cutting of the umbilical cord as my mate stared into the eyes of the child we had created.

"Is he okay?" I begged to know.

"He has ten perfect little fingers and ten perfect little toes. He has a tiny button nose that looks just like yours, and my mother's green eyes," Malcolm said with awe.

Mom moved me to the bed once everything was done and Malcolm came to sit beside me with our son wrapped in a white blanket. She peered down at him with pure joy on her face.

"He's perfect, Arista. You should be proud of that beautiful baby. I'll go tell your father."

I only had eyes for my son after that. His skin was perfectly pink, and every part of him appeared human. I knew Malcolm had a human form and the dragon form, but would our child?

"Is he…" I let my words trail off, glancing up at Malcolm.

"I think so, you see that gleam that keeps dancing through his eyes? I think he's a shifter."

"He must be if you two have been able to talk all of this time."

"I suppose you're right. Do you think we should give him a name now?" We'd wanted to wait until we met him before we named him.

"I think he's an Edward, don't you?"

"Hell no!" He'd picked that up from human television and it made me snort. "Edward? No, that won't do at all. What about Aelfric?"

"What the fu—no! Whatever that is, no!"

"George?" he offered, instead.

"No, that's not—" But then the world went dark and I didn't even know what my son's name was.

EPILOGUE

WILLOW

The sound of a crying infant pierced the quiet of the grove. I looked around at oak trees far more ancient than any I'd ever seen before. Their limbs were so old and thick that they rested on the ground. Green moss streamed from their top branches, and the breeze moaned through the forest.

I absorbed the scenery of the unfamiliar place, amazed at the beauty of where Malcolm's brother had brought me. Arista's child was crying in the distance, and I felt pity for a child that only wanted its mother. I studied the grove, feeling magic untamed as I turned away from the piercing cries. His father would be there to soothe him.

We'd all been terrified when she passed out soon after giving birth, but she'd soon awakened, refreshed and ready to name her child. Galen was the name they chose, because it meant peaceful and calm, just like their delightful little son. He was a beautiful child, and now his mother and father were getting married in the old way, in a grove filled with ancient magic.

"Willow," that voice called out my name.

I turned to see Henry there, waiting for me. He irritated me with his charming smile and his arrogant manners.

He was my mate, but that did not mean I had to like it. Arista thought I didn't know, but I did. He'd fascinated me the first time I saw him, but he'd begun to hang around to heal me and keep his own strength up, and I've come to find him irritating.

He was always talking about how rich he was, how he could buy anything he wanted, and he'd been all over the world. I had nothing to compare that with. I could get him a gallon of milk and show him the Wal Mart twenty miles away, but that was it.

His charming grin was in place, flashing at me as he found me alone in the grove.

"It's all ready then?" he asked me, and his gaze raked over me.

I felt the heat of desire but ignored it. I didn't want to feel desire for Henry, I just wanted to heal so I could get back to my real life and the real world. Arista might be getting her dream wedding, but that wasn't in my stars. I was meant for other things.

"Yes, as soon as the guests arrive," I spoke to him in a monotone voice, not inviting, but not telling him to piss off like I wanted to.

Not exactly, anyway.

"I'm going to have a wedding like this one day," he hinted, his eyes on me.

"That's only because of the—" but I stopped myself before I went too far.

Maybe if we weren't mates I'd feel differently, but we were. I wanted love because it was driven by passion and need, not a physiological reaction to something fate decreed. Would he feel the same if he wasn't my mate? Would he be dreaming of weddings and the future?

I was healed now. I wanted to get back to playing the piano and composing symphonies. I didn't want to think about babies and weddings.

He came close to me, his eyes burning into mine.

"You can have your symphonies, Willow, and you can have your passion, if only you'd give in to what we can't deny." His words were a confrontation, one I didn't want to have right now.

I pushed him away, or rather, I tried to, but my hands only drew him closer. His eyes were so beautiful, and his lips looked so inviting.

I felt a shiver go down my spine as his hands ran up my bare arms. I was wearing a white sleeveless dress as Arista had requested. Want filled me, and for the first time in my life, I didn't think I'd be able to say no to something. To Henry.

I moved closer to his lips, wondering how long it would be before the wedding guests arrived. Was there time to slip away, let him give me the physical satisfaction I craved, and then come back?

I waited, my lips parted in anticipation of this first kiss, trying to make a decision.

ALSO BY SELINA COFFEY

Shift Quickie

2 Hard To Bear

Bearly Over

Bearly Wolf

Kill Order

The Alpha

Kane

Cade

Jacob

Destiny Of The Dragon Prince

Defying The Dragon Prince

Chamber Of The Dragon Prince

His To Take

His to Mate

His To Save

and more...

ABOUT THE AUTHOR

Selina Coffey is a romance writer who lives happily in London with her husband and son. She is a hopeless romantic who grew up always believing in love and she is not ashamed to admit this! It is this belief that makes her so passionate about writing crazy love stories.

A stereotypical girly girl, she loves shopping. So whenever she gets a chance and the spare cash, you will probably find her browsing online for the next pair of shoes to add to her collection.!

You can find her online at
www.selinacoffey.com

Contact her at
hello@selinacoffey.com